"I Promise You W... Morgan Said.

"At least for the next two years?"

"At least," he said, nodding as he lowered his mouth to hers.

He didn't want to dwell on the length of their upcoming marriage, or the reason for it. At the moment, the feel of Samantha's soft body against his and the sound of her soft sigh were sending his libido into overdrive.

Tracing her lips with his tongue, Morgan deepened the kiss to leisurely reacquaint himself with her sweetness, to explore the woman who in two days would become his wife.

Knowing that if things went much further he wouldn't be able to stop, he broke the kiss and took a step back. "I…really should check on a new colt," he said, turning toward the back door. Without waiting for her response, he stepped out onto the porch and closed the door behind him.

Their marriage might not be a love match, but the attraction between them was too strong to be denied. There was no way the two of them could live in the same house, day in and day out, without the inevitable happening between them.

It wasn't a matter of if they made love. The question now was when?

Dear Reader,

Thanks for choosing Silhouette Desire, *the* place to find passionate, powerful and provocative love stories. We're starting off the month in style with Diana Palmer's *Man in Control,* a LONG, TALL TEXANS story and the author's 100th book! Congratulations, Diana, and thank you so much for each and every one of your wonderful stories.

Our continuing series DYNASTIES: THE BARONES is back this month with Anne Marie Winston's thrilling tale *Born To Be Wild.* And Cindy Gerard gives us a fabulous story about a woman who finds romance at her best friend's wedding, in *Tempting the Tycoon.* Weddings seem to be the place to meet a romantic partner (note to self: get invited to more weddings), as we find in Shawna Delacorte's *Having the Best Man's Baby.*

Also this month, Kathie DeNosky is back with another title in her ongoing ranching series—don't miss *Lonetree Ranchers: Morgan* and watch for the final story in this trilogy coming in December. Finally, welcome back the wonderful Emilie Rose with *Cowboy's Million-Dollar Secret,* a fantastic story about a man who inherits much more than he ever expected.

More passion to you!

Melissa Jeglinski

Melissa Jeglinski
Senior Editor
Silhouette Desire

Please address questions and book requests to:
Silhouette Reader Service
U.S.: 3010 Walden Ave., P.O. Box 1325, Buffalo, NY 14269
Canadian: P.O. Box 609, Fort Erie, Ont. L2A 5X3

Lonetree
Ranchers: Morgan
KATHIE DeNOSKY

Silhouette® Desire®

Published by Silhouette Books
America's Publisher of Contemporary Romance

SILHOUETTE BOOKS

ISBN 0-373-76540-1

LONETREE RANCHERS: MORGAN

Copyright © 2003 by Kathie DeNosky

All rights reserved. Except for use in any review, the reproduction or utilization of this work in whole or in part in any form by any electronic, mechanical or other means, now known or hereafter invented, including xerography, photocopying and recording, or in any information storage or retrieval system, is forbidden without the written permission of the editorial office, Silhouette Books, 233 Broadway, New York, NY 10279 U.S.A.

All characters in this book have no existence outside the imagination of the author and have no relation whatsoever to anyone bearing the same name or names. They are not even distantly inspired by any individual known or unknown to the author, and all incidents are pure invention.

This edition published by arrangement with Harlequin Books S.A.

® and TM are trademarks of Harlequin Books S.A., used under license. Trademarks indicated with ® are registered in the United States Patent and Trademark Office, the Canadian Trade Marks Office and in other countries.

Visit Silhouette at www.eHarlequin.com

Printed in U.S.A.

KATHIE DᴇNOSKY

lives in her native southern Illinois with her husband, three children and one very spoiled Jack Russell terrier. She writes highly sensual stories with a generous amount of humor. Kathie's books have appeared on the Waldenbooks bestseller list and received the Write Touch Readers' Award from WisRWA and the National Readers' Choice Award. She enjoys going to rodeos, traveling to research settings for her books and listening to country music. She often works through the night so she can write without interruption while the rest of the family is sleeping. You may contact Kathie at P.O. Box 2064, Herrin, Illinois 62948-5264 or e-mail her at kathie@kathiedenosky.com.

To Charlie, who puts up with my odd hours
and loves me anyway.

And a very special thank-you
to the Professional Bull Riders.

One

"**W**hat the hell do you think you're doing in here?"

In the process of building a fire in the big stone fireplace, Samantha Peterson jumped and spun around at the sound of the man's angry voice and the old wooden door slamming back against the wall. The biggest cowboy she'd ever seen stood like a tree rooted in the middle of the threshold. Lightning flashed outside behind him and every story she'd ever heard about the bogeyman flooded her mind.

His eyes were hidden by the wide brim of his black cowboy hat pulled down low on his forehead, but if the grim set of his mouth was any indication, he was not only the biggest cowboy she'd ever seen, he was also the angriest. He took a step forward at the same time a gust of wind whipped his long black coat around his legs. That's when Samantha noticed he held a rifle in one big gloved hand.

"I…I'm…ooh—" Samantha bent forward slightly, squeezed her eyes shut and groaned from the sudden tightness gripping her stomach.

"Good God, you're pregnant!" He sounded shocked.

Anger coursed through her. He'd scared the bejeebers out of her and all he had to say was, "You're pregnant?"

"Thank you for informing me…of that fact," she said through clenched teeth. "I doubt that I'd…have noticed otherwise."

"Are you all right?"

His voice sounded too close for comfort, but that was the least of Samantha's concerns. She had a feeling this wasn't one of the Braxton-Hicks contractions that she'd been experiencing for the past couple of weeks. It felt too different to be false labor. This felt like it might be the real thing. But that wasn't possible, was it? She still had three weeks before she reached her due date.

"No, I'm not all right," she said as the tight feeling decreased. Ready to give the man a piece of her mind, she straightened to her full height. "You scared the living daylights…"

Her voice trailed off as she looked up—way up—at the man standing next to her. The sheer size of him sent a shiver of apprehension slithering up her spine and had her stepping away from him. The top of her head barely reached his chin. At five foot six, she wasn't an Amazon by any means, but she wasn't short either. But this man was at least ten inches taller and appeared to be extremely muscular.

"Look, I'm sorry I yelled," he said, his deep baritone sending another tremor through her that had nothing whatsoever to do with fear. "I expected to find one of the local teenage boys getting ready to throw one of his Saturday night beer busts."

"As you can see, I'm not a teenage boy." Samantha moved away a couple of extra steps. She needed to put more distance between them, in case a fast getaway was in order. At least, as fast as her advanced pregnancy would allow. "And I can assure you, I'm not getting ready to throw a drinking party."

His mouth curved up in a smile and he used his thumb to push the wide brim of his cowboy hat up, revealing the most startling blue eyes she'd ever seen. "Let's start over." He extended his big hand. "I'm Morgan Wakefield."

When she cautiously placed her hand in his, his fingers closed around hers and a warm tingle raced through her. As he stared at her expectantly, she had trouble finding her voice. "I'm, uh, Samantha Peterson," she finally managed as she tugged her hand from his.

"Nice to meet you, Mrs. Peterson."

"That's *Ms.* Peterson," Samantha corrected. "I'm not married."

His gaze traveled to her swollen stomach, then back to her face before he gave her a short nod. Had that been a hint of disapproval she'd detected in his expression just before he gave her a bland smile?

If so, that was just too darned bad. It was none of his business whether she was married or not.

As they continued to stare wordlessly at each other, the sound of dripping water drew their attention to the corner of the room. Hurrying into the kitchen, Samantha rummaged through the cabinets until she found a large pot.

When she returned to the living room, she shoved it under the steady stream of water pouring from the ceiling. "That's just great. Not even the roof on this place is in decent repair."

She watched Morgan Wakefield's eyes narrow. "Why do you care if the roof leaks or not?" he asked slowly.

"I was hoping it would at least keep me dry tonight," she said, gazing at the rain water collecting in the pot.

"You're staying? Here? Tonight?"

"Yes. Yes. And yes," she said, smiling at his incredulous look. "I inherited it from my grandfather."

"You're Tug Shackley's granddaughter?"

Samantha nodded and walked over to the wide stone hearth to slowly lower herself to a sitting position. Another contraction was building, and making sure to keep her breathing deep and even, she focused on relaxing every muscle in her body.

When it passed, she looked up to find that Morgan had propped his rifle against the armchair and stood with his hands on his narrow hips. He was watching her as if he didn't quite know what to think. "Are you sure you're all right?"

"Yes. I'll be fine just as soon as I have my baby," she said, reminding herself to stay calm, even though the baby was coming earlier than expected. "Do you happen to know where the nearest hospital is?"

If the widening of his vivid blue eyes was any indication, it had been the last thing he'd expected her to ask. "Oh hell, lady. You're not—"

"Yes, I am." She almost laughed at the horrified expression that crossed his handsome face. "Now, if you'll answer my question concerning the location of the nearest hospital, I'll get in my car and go have my baby."

He removed his hat and ran an agitated hand through his shiny sable-black hair. "You can't drive yourself to the hospital."

"And why not, Mr. Wakefield?" she asked, staring up at him.

Not only was he one of the biggest men she'd ever met, he was one of the best-looking. He had a small white scar above his right eyebrow and his lean cheeks sported a day's growth of beard, but it only added to his rugged appeal.

"The name's Morgan," he said, jamming his hat back on his head. "And it's not safe for you to be driving in your condition. What if the pain caused you to run off the road?''

Samantha awkwardly pushed herself to her feet. ''That's a chance I'll have to take. Now, if you'll excuse me, we'll have to get acquainted some other time. Right now, I have to go deliver my baby.''

He stubbornly shook his head. ''Where's your car parked?''

''In the garage, or shed, or whatever you want to call that dilapidated thing behind the house.'' She collected her shoulder bag from the mantel. ''Why?''

''The nearest hospital is over sixty miles from here, in Laramie.'' He held out his hand. ''Give me your keys and I'll drive you down there.''

''That's not necessary,'' she said, shaking her head. ''I'm perfectly capable of—''

Arguing with Morgan, she was unprepared for the contraction that wrapped around her belly and seemed to squeeze the breath out of her. When she dropped her purse and bent double, he caught her by the shoulders and supported her until the feeling eased.

''You can't even stand up when the pain hits.'' He picked up her purse and held it out to her. ''Now, give me your keys and I'll go get your car.''

As much as she hated to admit it, he was right. Digging in her purse, she handed him the keys to her twenty-year-old Ford. ''You might have trouble starting it. It's kind of tricky sometimes. I think it might need a tune-up.''

''Don't worry. I think I can handle starting a car,''

Morgan said dryly. Taking the keys from her, he turned toward the door, but stopped abruptly when she started to follow. ''There's no sense in both of us getting drenched. Stay inside until I get the car pulled up closer to the porch, then I'll help you down the steps.''

''I think I can navigate a set of steps by myself,'' she argued.

''They aren't in the best repair and I don't think you want to deal with a broken leg, in addition to having a baby.''

He left the house before she could argue the point further and sprinted across the yard. He'd waited for this day for almost eighteen months. Tug's heir had finally been found. Unfortunately, she had the idea that she was going to take up residence in the place. And at the moment, she for damned sure wasn't in any shape to listen to his arguments about why she should sell it to him, instead of carrying out her plan of moving in.

He almost laughed as he folded his tall frame into the driver's seat of the compact car. Women. Where did they get these empty-headed ideas anyway? She'd have to be blind not to see that it would take more money than it was worth to fix up this dump.

Inserting the key into the ignition, he turned it and the dull clicking sound that followed sent a chill racing up his spine. He glanced at the dashboard. There wasn't one of the indicator lights lit. He closed his eyes in frustration and barely resisted the urge to pound on the dash with his fist. The battery was as dead as poor old Tug.

When he climbed out of the bucket seat and raised the hood, he rattled off a string of cuss words that would have done a sailor proud. The battery terminals were so covered with corrosion he wouldn't be surprised to see that it had eaten through the cables. He looked around for something to knock some of the oxidation loose, but abandoned that idea immediately. Even if he got rid of most of the crud without breaking the contacts, there was no way to charge the damned thing. He slammed the hood back down with force.

Desperation clawed at his insides as the gravity of the situation settled over him. The only way to get help would involve him riding his horse back to the Lonetree through a pouring rain to get his truck. That would take at least thirty minutes going across country. Then it would take another forty-five minutes to drive the road between the two ranches.

Morgan shook his head as he stared at the sheet of rain just outside the shed's double doors. Riding through a downpour didn't bother him. Hell, he'd done that more times than he cared to count. But the creek between his ranch and this one always flooded when it rained this hard, and it would be impossible to cross now. He could use the road, but that would take a couple of hours to get back to her, and he didn't like the idea of leaving a pregnant woman—a woman in labor, no less—by herself. And he'd bet his right arm that she wouldn't be any crazier about his leaving her alone than he was.

For the first time since meeting Samantha Peterson, he allowed himself to think about his first impression of her. Her golden-brown hair framed a face that could easily grace the cover of a glamour magazine. But her eyes were what had damned near knocked him to his knees when he'd first seen her standing by the fireplace. Whiskey-brown with flecks of gold, they'd made him think of hot sultry nights and long hours of passionate sex.

Morgan sucked in a sharp breath. Now where the hell had that come from?

He cussed a blue streak. It had been quite a while since he'd enjoyed the warmth of a woman's body and the long dry spell was beginning to take its toll. What he needed was a trip to Buffalo Gals Saloon down in Bear Creek for a night of good old-fashioned hell-raising. He was sure to find a willing little filly down there to help him scratch his itch and forget how lonely the long Wyoming winter had been.

Shaking his head, he turned his attention back to the matters at hand. Now was not the time to lament how sorry his sex life was. What he and Samantha Peterson were facing right now was a lot more important.

A sinking feeling settled over him as he reviewed the options to their present dilemma. He might as well accept the inevitable and start preparing for what had to be done. Within the next few hours, he was going to have to add the delivery of a baby to his arsenal of emergency medical skills. Unless, of course, by some miracle someone else showed up. And the chances of that happening were slim to none.

Sighing heavily, he turned back to her car, opened the trunk and rummaged around until he found what he was looking for. Gathering pillows, sheets, blankets and towels, he ran back to the house.

By the time he walked through the door, Samantha sat on the hearth with her gaze transfixed on the faded picture hanging on the opposite wall. She looked as if she was in some kind of daze and he wondered if she might be going into shock.

But as he mentally reviewed what he knew about treating shock victims, she took a deep breath, slowly blew it out, then looked at him expectantly. "Are we ready to go?" she asked, rising to her feet as if nothing had happened.

Relieved that she seemed to be all right, he shook his head and tried to think of a way to break the news as gently as he could. He sighed heavily. Some things just couldn't be sugar-coated.

"The battery's dead. I'm afraid we're stuck here for a while."

Her pretty amber eyes widened considerably as she looked around the room. "But I have to go to the hospital. There's no doctor here. What if…I mean the baby is early. There might be a need for—"

Walking over to her, Morgan placed his hands on her shoulders. The last thing he needed right now was for her to go into a blind panic. "Take a deep breath and listen to me, Samantha. You're not alone. I'm here."

"Are you a doctor?" Her expressive eyes begged him to say that he was.

At the moment, Morgan would have given everything he owned for a medical degree. "No, I'm not," he answered truthfully. "But we'll get through this. You've got my word on that." He just hoped liked hell he could live up to the promise.

"What about your car, or truck, or whatever you came in?" she asked hopefully. "Can't we use that?"

He ran his hand over the back of his neck in an effort to ease some of the mounting tension and shook his head. "I rode my horse. Getting back to the Lonetree, then driving back here in my truck, would take hours."

"Your horse," she repeated, looking more apprehensive by the second.

"I tied it in the barn when I arrived," he said, hoping she didn't get hysterical.

She brightened suddenly, as if she had the answer to the immediate problem. "What about a cell phone? Everyone has a cell phone these days. You can't go to a movie or out to dinner without hearing one ring."

"I have one, but certain areas of this region are dead zones," he explained. "This is one of them. Even if I'd bothered to bring it with me, it would be useless without a signal."

She opened her mouth to say something, but instead of words she let loose with a low moan. The hair on the back of his neck stood straight up and his gut twisted into a tight knot. When she began to fold, Morgan pulled her to him and supported her weight while the pain held her in its grip.

Sweat popped out on his forehead and upper lip. This was going to be hard as hell to deal with. He didn't like seeing anything in pain, and definitely not a woman. He'd rather climb a barbed wire fence buck naked than to see a female in pain.

How was he going to handle Samantha going through hours of labor and not be able to do a damned thing but watch? And what if things didn't go like they were supposed to?

He swallowed around the lump forming in his throat. He knew all too well what could happen if something went wrong. At the age of seven he'd lost his own mother because of complications during the birth of his youngest brother, Colt. And she'd been in the hospital.

The pain ebbed and the woman he held took a deep breath. "I've got to maintain my focus," she said, sounding determined. "It will make all of this much easier if I can do that."

Morgan wasn't sure if she was trying to convince him or herself. But at the moment, it didn't matter. His biggest concern was to get her off her feet, make sure she was as comfortable as possible, then start gathering some of the supplies he'd need.

"Why don't you sit by the fire while I get the

couch pulled over here for you to lie down?'' he asked, helping her lower herself to the raised stone hearth.

''You, um, haven't by any chance done this before, have you?'' she asked. Her hopeful tone caused the knot in his gut to tighten.

He refrained from answering as he pulled the drop cloth from the dingy green couch, threw it onto a chair and shoved the heavy piece of furniture closer to the warmth of the fire. He'd delivered hundreds, maybe thousands, of babies in his lifetime. But none of them had been human. And somehow, he didn't think Samantha Peterson would be all that impressed with his expertise as a bovine obstetrician. With any luck she wouldn't ask him again, and he wouldn't have to tell her.

''Well, have you?'' she persisted.

Morgan almost groaned out loud. Why couldn't she just drop it and accept the inevitable? He was the best—the only—source of help she was going to get.

''Yes, and no.'' He unfolded one of the sheets he'd retrieved from her car and arranged it over the sagging piece of furniture, along with a couple of pillows. ''If you count the calves and colts I've delivered, yes, I've done this before.'' He helped her up from the hearth and over to the couch. ''If not, then no, I haven't.''

She sat down suddenly and went into that trance-like state that she'd been in when he'd come in from trying to start the car. Fascinated, he watched her take deep, rhythmic breaths and lightly massage her swollen belly as she stared at the brim of his hat. Her porcelain cheeks colored a deep rose, but her determination to ride out the pain was evident in the set of her stubborn little chin and her unwavering concentration.

When she came out of the daze, she looked up at him and continued talking as if nothing had happened. It was the damnedest thing he'd ever witnessed.

"There's a book on pregnancy in my handbag. I think it has emergency delivery instructions and a list of things you'll need." She nervously caught her lower lip between her teeth before she continued, "I hope you're a quick study."

If there was one thing Morgan admired, and a sure-fire way of judging what a person was made of, it was watching how they handled themselves in a tense situation. And he'd have to give credit where it was due. The little lady settling herself back against the pillows on the sagging green couch had her share of grit.

He could tell by the shadows in her pretty whiskey-colored eyes that she was scared witless. But the firm set of her perfectly shaped mouth indicated that she wasn't going to panic. Whatever came their way, she was going to deal with it.

Giving her the most reassuring smile he was capable of under the circumstances, Morgan handed her the oversized purse. "You find that book. I'll take care of the rest."

She pulled the book from the depths of the bag,

then, shoving it into his hands, went back into another one of her trances. While she took deep, even breaths and stared off into space, he quickly scanned the index of the book she'd given him for instructions on an emergency, at-home delivery.

Turning to the page the directory had indicated, he read the first entry. Calling 9-1-1 was out of the question. He skipped down to the second directive—if possible call for help.

Well hell, that was a no-brainer. If he could call someone else to assist, he'd call 9-1-1.

When his gaze dropped to the third instruction, he swallowed hard and glanced at her as she came back from wherever she went in her mind to escape the pain.

"What?" she asked when he continued to stare at her.

He cleared his throat. There was no easy way of breaking news like this to a woman he'd known for— he checked his watch—a little less than an hour.

"It says you need to strip from the waist down," he finally answered, making sure to keep his voice even and his gaze steady.

"Is that necessary right now?" she asked just as calmly. He wasn't sure, but it looked as if her already flushed cheeks turned a deeper shade of crimson.

Shrugging, Morgan handed her the book and walked into the kitchen to find another pot. He needed to get some water boiling in order to sterilize a few things he would have to use during the delivery. And she needed to come to grips with the way things had to be.

When he walked back into the living room on his way to set a couple of pots outside to collect rainwater for boiling, he noticed that she'd used one of the blankets he'd brought in from the car to drape over her lap. Glancing to the end of the couch, he saw that her jeans were neatly folded on the arm, while her tennis shoes and socks sat on the floor beside it. She didn't look his way and he didn't comment on the fact that she'd obviously done as the book had indicated.

"Would you feel better lying down?" he asked when he returned from placing the pots on the porch steps.

She shook her head. "Not yet."

Sweat beaded her forehead as she handed him the book and, once again, focused her energy on riding the current wave of pain. Standing there watching her, Morgan had never felt more useless in his entire life. He wanted to help her, but he didn't have a clue how to go about it.

Needing to do something, anything, he turned to the woodbox by the fireplace, removed several logs, then carefully stacked them on the dying fire in the grate. Even though it was early May, and fairly warm, there was a damp chill to the room, and he figured he would need all the light he could get when the time came for the baby's grand entrance. Besides, he needed something to keep himself busy in order to take his mind off what Samantha was going through.

The dry wood caught immediately and the fire

blazed high, chasing away the approaching shadows of late afternoon. He shrugged out of his duster and tossing it toward the chair where he'd thrown the drop cloth, went in search of some other source of light. Fortunately, he found two kerosene lamps in the pantry with full reservoirs. He returned to the living room, placed them on the mantel and lit the wicks with some stick matches he'd found in the kitchen, then sat on the hearth and picked up the book. Running his finger down the list of preparations, he glanced up. Where the hell was he going to find two pieces of sturdy string to tie off the cord?

He scanned the room, then zeroed in on Samantha's tennis shoes sitting where she'd placed them by the end of the couch. Her shoe laces would have to do. He checked the book again. It didn't say anything about sterilizing what he used to tie the cord, but he figured it couldn't hurt. Just to be on the safe side, he'd toss them in the boiling water along with his pocket knife. Even if the hot water caused them to shrink, they should still be long enough for what he needed.

He laid the book within easy reach, then stood up and unfastened the cuffs of his chambray shirt. Rolling the long sleeves to the middle of his forearms, he waited for Samantha to relax her intense focus.

"The book says we need to start timing your contractions in order to tell how you're progressing. Let me know when you feel another one coming on."

She nodded. "They're coming closer together."

They were getting stronger, too. That much he

could tell from the tiny strain lines bracketing her mouth. On impulse he reached out and took her hand in his. Giving it a gentle squeeze, he tried to reassure her. "You're going to do just fine, Samantha."

She squeezed back. "Remind me of that in a few hours."

"Will do," he said, nodding. He had no idea why the trust she was placing in him caused his chest to swell, but it did. Deciding that he could analyze what it meant later, he released her hand and started for the door. "I'll be right back. I'm going to go get the rainwater I've been collecting so that I can put it on the fire to boil."

"Morgan?"

The sound of his name on her soft voice sent a tingle up his spine. He swallowed hard and turned back to face her. "What, Samantha?"

"Thank you for being so calm. It really helps." The look she gave him clearly stated that she was counting on him to get her through whatever happened.

At a loss for words, he nodded and walked out to the porch to get the pots of water. Samantha had no way of knowing that his insides were churning like a damned cement mixer from thoughts of all the things that could go wrong, as they had with his mother.

Morgan took a deep breath, then slowly released it. And if it was the last thing he ever did, he had no intention of letting her find out.

Two

Four hours later, Morgan sat on the hearth in front of Samantha where she perched on the edge of the couch. For the last hour he'd watched her alternate between sitting forward and leaning back against the pillows in her effort to get comfortable. She had his hand in a death grip as she rode the current wave of pain and it surprised him how strong she was. It felt more like a lumberjack had a hold of his hand than a woman, and her nails digging into his palm felt as if she might draw blood. But if it helped her get through this, he'd gladly let her rip the skin clean off.

As he watched her stare off into space and pant her way through the contraction, his admiration for her grew by leaps and bounds. She was in tremendous pain, but her determination to stay on top of it, to ride it out, was amazing.

He was sure she was in what the book called "active labor" because of the duration of her contractions and the time between them. He glanced at his watch. They still had the "transitional labor" to go through and, if the book was right, they probably had another couple of hours before they got to the actual delivery. He just hoped he could last that long. With every contraction Samantha had, his gut twisted tighter and he felt a little more helpless than he had only moments before.

When she blew out a deep breath, signaling that the contraction had ended, he asked, "Is there anything else I can do? The book says that you might have some back pain? Do you need your back rubbed?"

"Would you mind?" she asked, releasing his hand. She winced. "My back is killing me."

Removing his Resistol, Morgan sailed it like a Frisbee to land on the chair with his duster, took a deep breath and eased over to sit next to her on the ugly green couch. He slipped his hand beneath her pink T-shirt to lightly kneed the muscles of her lower back, and valiantly tried to ignore the fact that her skin felt like satin beneath his callused palm. Now was not the time for him to remember how much he missed the way a woman's softness felt.

"Is it helping?" he asked.

"A little." She suddenly took a deep breath and once again focused on riding out another pain.

Morgan continued to rub her back with his right hand as he glanced at the watch on his left wrist. This contraction had come a lot faster than the last one. He watched the second hand sweep around once, then halfway around again before Samantha blew out a deep breath, signaling it was over.

"Stop touching me," she said sharply. "You're making it worse."

"Okay," he said, removing his hand from beneath her shirt. He knew for certain that he hadn't rubbed her back *that* hard.

Frowning, Morgan moved back to the hearth and picked up the book. Unless he missed his guess, they were moving on to the next step.

Yep. Sure as shootin', Samantha had all the signs of a woman in "transitional labor." She'd suddenly become as irritable as a bear with a sore paw, didn't want to be touched, and the most telling of the symptoms was the duration of the last contraction.

He wiped the sweat from his forehead and watched her struggle to stay focused as the next wave of pain hit her. Her face was flushed, her golden-brown hair hung in damp tendrils from perspiration and the lines of strain around her mouth had deepened.

He'd never felt more useless.

When she blew out a deep breath, he laid the book aside and wiped her face with a cool damp washcloth.

Her gaze met his, and it was damned near his undoing when tears filled her pretty amber eyes.

"I don't think…I can't do this, Morgan."

Making sure the book was within easy reach, Morgan took her hands in his. "You're doing just fine, Samantha." The instructions had indicated that he should encourage her and help her stay focused. He wasn't sure how the hell to go about that, but he'd do it or die trying. "You're in the home stretch, sweetheart. It won't be much longer."

He watched her eyes cloud with pain, felt her hands tighten on his in a death grip. She started to say something, but a moan came out instead.

It tore him apart to see her hurting and not be able to do anything to help. "Look at me, Samantha."

Her breathing ragged, she shook her head. "This is…too hard," she said, her voice cracking.

"Come on, Samantha, look at me," he said more firmly.

When she finally did as he commanded, Morgan nodded. "That's it, sweetheart. Stay focused and squeeze my hands as hard as you can. Concentrate on transferring the pain to me."

He wasn't sure if the book supported his way of taking her mind off the contraction, but he didn't care. All that mattered was that it seemed to be working. Samantha held his gaze and damned near cut off the circulation to his fingers as she tightened her hands on his.

What seemed like an eternity, but couldn't have

been more than a couple of minutes later, she suddenly released his hands to lay back against the couch. ''I need to push.''

The hair on the back of Morgan's neck shot straight up and his stomach did a back-flip. ''Are you sure?'' he asked, flexing his fingers in an effort to return the circulation.

Nodding, she scrunched her eyes shut, grabbed her knees with her hands and pushed with all her might.

Morgan wanted to run like hell. Instead, he grabbed the book, quickly read what he needed to do, then prayed like he'd never prayed before.

He could do this. Along with his dad and brothers, he'd played baby doctor to the herds of Lonetree cattle for as long as he could remember. Surely he could deliver one little human baby.

Placing the book within easy reach, he washed his hands in one of the pots of water that he'd boiled earlier, then fished his sterilized pocket knife and Samantha's shoelaces from the other. Fortunately, the water had cooled enough that it wasn't scalding, but it was still damned hot. His mind on what was about to take place, he barely noticed.

To Morgan, the next thirty minutes seemed to pass in a fast-forward blur. Samantha worked hard to push her baby out into the world as he uttered words he hoped were encouraging. Then, just after midnight, a little baby boy with dark brown hair slid out into his waiting hands, opened his mouth and started yowling at the top of his tiny lungs.

A lump the size of his fist formed in Morgan's throat as he stared down at the child he'd helped to enter the world. Awed by the miracle he'd participated in, he couldn't have strung two words together if his life depended on it.

"Is my baby all right?" Samantha asked, sounding stronger than he would have thought possible after what she'd been through.

Relieved that things had turned out the way they should, Morgan tied off the cord in two places, cut it between the ties, then wrapped the baby in fluffy towels. His hands shaking slightly, he placed the infant in her waiting arms.

Clearing his throat, he finally managed, "I'm not a doctor, but he looks normal to me." He grinned. "If his squalling is any indication, I'd say he's mad as hell about this whole birthing business though."

"He's beautiful." He watched tears fill Samantha's eyes as she glanced up at him. "I can't thank you enough for helping us, Morgan."

"You did all the work." Finishing the last of what the instructions indicated should be done, he washed up and rolled his sleeves back down to fasten them at his wrists. "Have you picked out a name for him?"

The smile she gave him made Morgan feel as if the sun had broken through on a gray, cloudy day. "As a matter of fact, I think I have," she said softly. "How does Timothy *Morgan* Peterson sound?"

Two days later, Samantha sat on the side of her hospital bed, staring at the discharge papers the nurse had handed her only moments ago. Now what? Where were she and the baby supposed to go? And how were they supposed to get there?

She didn't have her car. And even if she did, it wouldn't run. The morning after Timmy had been born, Morgan rode his horse back to his ranch, then drove over to her grandfather's place in his truck to take her and the baby to the hospital.

She sighed as she looked at her son sleeping peacefully in the bassinet. She could call a cab. But where would she have it take her and Timmy? She certainly couldn't afford the fare for a sixty mile trip back to her newly inherited ranch. She shook her head. Make that her newly inherited dump.

"Do you need help getting dressed?" the nurse asked, strolling back into the room with a complimentary bag of sample baby products. She picked up Timmy from the tiny bed to wrap him in a soft, baby blue receiving blanket. "By the way, I caught your husband in the hall and told him you two were ready to leave."

Dumbfounded, Samantha blinked. "My husband?" The woman had to have confused her with another new mother. "I'm not—"

"I sent him to bring his truck around to the front entrance," the woman said as if Samantha hadn't spoken. "Once you're dressed, I'll get a wheelchair and you and this little darling can be on your way."

"But I still have to go down to the business office to make arrangements to pay the bill. And I'm not—"

"Don't worry, Samantha. It's taken care of," Morgan said, walking through the doorway as if he owned the place. He handed her a shopping bag. "All you have to do is put these clothes on and we can get out of here."

"I'll get the wheelchair," the nurse said, her shoes making a whispering sound against the tiled floor as she quickly left the room.

Samantha stared at the man who had been her rock throughout the birth of her child. He was without a doubt one of the best-looking men she'd ever seen. And apparently one of the most arrogant.

"What do you mean it's taken care of?" she demanded. She wasn't sure what he'd done, but she had a feeling she wasn't going to like it when she found out.

"We'll talk about it on the drive home."

"I think we'd better discuss this right now," she said flatly. She wasn't going anywhere until he told her what was going on.

Completely ignoring her protest, he took the shopping bag from her stiff fingers, opened it and pulled out a cream-colored T-shirt and denim jumper. "I wasn't sure about the size, so I had a clerk pick out everything. She said these were 'one size fits most'— whatever that means." He looked a little unsure as he shoved them into her hands and turned to leave. "Go ahead and get dressed so we can get out of here. I'll be waiting with the truck when the nurse brings you out the front entrance."

"Morgan, I want to know what—"

"I don't want to argue with you, Samantha," he interrupted. "It's not good for you, and I really don't have time for it. I'd like to get back to the Lonetree by lunchtime. So get dressed and I'll meet you out front."

Before she could demand answers, he grabbed the small overnight case she'd brought with her to the hospital, turned and left the room, leaving her to stare after him. She needed to get back to her grandfather's ranch—make that hers now—to see about her car. And with very little money, she really didn't have any other options of getting there.

She sighed heavily, then removing the tags from the jumper and T-shirt, slipped the pieces of light-weight cardboard into her purse. She wasn't a charity case. As soon as she could, she'd pay Morgan back for the clothes.

Hurriedly changing from the hospital gown, she hardened her resolve to find out what he meant about the hospital bill being taken care of. They had a good sixty mile drive ahead of them, and if he'd done what she suspected, they were going to have a long talk on the way. A *really* long talk.

Fifteen minutes later, when the nurse guided the wheelchair through the double glass doors of the hospital's front entrance, Morgan was leaning against the fender of his shiny silver-gray truck, his arms folded across his chest, boots crossed at the ankles. His denim jacket emphasized the width of his shoulders and his well-worn jeans hugged his muscular thighs like a second skin. She gulped. He looked like every woman's fantasy—rugged, handsome and thoroughly masculine.

When he saw her, he smiled as he straightened to his full height and opened the passenger door of the shiny pickup. A tiny shiver coursed through her when his hand brushed her breast as he reached to take Timmy.

''You three make a nice little family,'' the nurse said, watching Morgan cradle the baby with one arm, while he helped Samantha up onto the bench seat with the other. ''Have a safe trip home.''

''Thanks. We'll do that,'' he said, handing the baby to Samantha. He closed the door of the truck before she could correct the nurse about them being a family.

''Why didn't you tell her we aren't together?'' Samantha demanded when he slid into the driver's seat and turned the key in the ignition.

''It just seemed faster and a whole hell of a lot easier than explaining the situation,'' he answered, shrugging one shoulder.

She fastened the seat belt over the car seat she'd had him get from her car the day before when he'd brought her and the baby to the hospital to be checked over. ''You don't approve of my having a child without a husband, do you?''

''I can't say that I do, or don't,'' he said, putting the truck into gear. He steered it out onto the street, then glancing at her, added, "Samantha, I don't know the circumstances." His expression turned grim. "But the baby's father should have been here to help you through this."

She watched the easy way Morgan handled the big truck as he navigated the traffic. He was a man in complete control, and one who could be counted on in any situation. Unlike Timmy's father.

Her chest tightened at the thought of the man who'd fathered a child he cared nothing about. How could she have been so wrong about Chad?

When they first started living together, they'd both worked at achieving the true give and take of a successful relationship. But six months later, Samantha suddenly realized that things had changed between them. She'd been the one doing all of the giving and he'd been the one doing the taking. Then one day she'd come home from work to find that he'd moved to L.A. to pursue his dream of becoming a musician. That's when she realized how shallow and uncaring Chad really was. He hadn't even bothered to face her to tell her things were over between them. He'd left a rather impersonal note stuck to the front of the refrigerator, saying that he'd had fun, but that it was time for him to move on.

"There's really not that much to tell," she found herself saying. Why Morgan's opinion mattered, she had no idea. But for some reason she wanted him to know that the choice to handle everything on her own, hadn't been hers. "We weren't married, and I didn't find out I was pregnant until after he and I had parted company."

She watched Morgan's hands tighten on the steering wheel, and she knew what he was thinking before he even asked, "He doesn't know about the baby?"

"Oh, I told him," she said, trying to keep her voice even. She would not allow herself to dwell on how hurt she'd been by Chad's decision. "I didn't ask him for any kind of help when I told him. I just thought he should know he'd fathered a baby, and that he might want to be part of Timmy's life. But he wasn't interested in knowing his child now, or in the future. He offered to sign away all legal rights to Timmy, and I accepted. End of story."

"Why would he do a dumb-ass thing like that?" Morgan asked bluntly. He shot her a scowl that stated quite clearly what he thought of Chad, and she knew beyond a shadow of doubt that it would be the last thing he'd do in the same situation.

Gazing down at her sleeping son, Samantha blinked back the threatening tears. "I suspect he thought it would insure that I'd never ask for any kind of financial help from him."

Morgan snorted. "I think a man who shirks his responsibilities and denies his child should be shot."

Samantha swallowed around the lump in her throat. "I think Timmy and I are better off this way."

"How do you figure that?" Morgan asked, clearly unable to comprehend her reasoning.

"Chad turned out to be very selfish and self-centered," she answered, gently touching her son's soft cheek. She took a deep breath to chase away the sadness she always felt when she thought of all that Timmy would miss by not having a father. "Why would I want a man like that helping me raise my son? It's not the kind of example I want set before Timmy. Besides, he deserves a father who loves him unconditionally, not one who simply views him as a monthly support check."

Morgan was silent for several long moments before he nodded. "I couldn't agree more. But when a man gets a woman pregnant, whether he ever sees the child or not, he has an obligation to help her."

Reaching the outskirts of Laramie, he set the cruise control, then stretched his right arm out along the back of the seat. His fingers brushed her hair and she felt warmed all the way to her toes.

Startled by her reaction, Samantha scooted over to lean against the door. "I have a question," she said, determined to regain her equilibrium.

He glanced her way and smiled. "And that would be?"

His easy expression caused her pulse to skip a beat. She took a deep breath to chase away her accompanying breathlessness. "When you walked into my room back at the hospital, you said everything had been taken care of at the business office. What did you mean?"

"Just that," he said, staring at the road ahead. "The bill is paid."

Samantha felt her stomach start to churn. "Would you like to tell me who paid it?"

"I did."

Anger swept through her. "Why?"

"Call it a baby gift," he said, his smile so darned charming that she had to fight the warmth filling her chest.

She shook her head as she tried desperately to hang on to her anger. "A baby gift is a high chair, a blanket, a set of bibs. It's *not* paying a hospital bill."

His smiled faded and a muscle began to work along his lean jaw. "Look, Samantha. I've got the money, and I don't mind helping out."

"I don't need your help," she said stubbornly. "I'm not a charity case."

He shook his head. "I never said you were."

"How much was the bill?" Reaching into her purse, she removed a pad of paper and a pen. "I'll reimburse you as soon as I find a job."

"No, you won't."

"Yes, I will."

"Dammit, woman." He looked exasperated. "I said no."

"You're used to people doing what you tell them to do, aren't you?" she asked, already knowing the answer.

He shrugged, but remained silent.

"Well, let me treat you to a reality check, cowboy.'' She stuffed the paper and pen back into her handbag. ''I've been on my own since I was eighteen. I make my own decisions and I pay my own way.''

As she glared at Morgan, the baby suddenly opened his eyes, waved his little fists in protest and wailed at the top of his lungs. Their raised voices had startled him.

''Why don't we put this argument on hold until we get home?'' Morgan asked, steering the truck off the main road.

Samantha quieted the baby, then looking around at the scenery, she frowned. Nothing looked familiar and she knew for certain they hadn't traveled this road when Morgan had taken her and Timmy to the hospital the day before.

''Where are we going?'' she asked, noticing the neatly fenced pastures on either side of the road.

''I'm taking you to the Lonetree,'' he said, as if that explained everything.

''Do you need to pick up something before you take me to my place?'' she asked cautiously.

''No.''

A knot of suspicion began to form in the pit of her stomach. ''Then why are we—''

''I thought you and the baby should stay at my ranch for a few days,'' he said, turning onto another road.

She shook her head vehemently. ''I most certainly will not be staying at your ranch.''

''Don't be stubborn about this, Samantha. Your

grandfather's house isn't in any shape for you and the baby to stay there.'' He made it sound so darned reasonable, she wanted to scream.

But as she thought about what he'd just said, some of her anger drained away. She hated to admit it, but Morgan was right. The house only had a fireplace in the living room for heat, there was no running water and no electricity. Besides all that, the roof leaked.

Frustrated beyond words, Samantha had to fight the sudden urge to cry. It just brought home how low her circumstances had become. For all intents and purposes, she was as homeless as the foster child she'd been after her mother passed away.

Slowing the truck to a stop, Morgan turned to face her. ''I understand how much you value your independence, sweetheart. And I swear I'm not trying to take that away from you. But you have to be realistic about this.'' He reached over the car seat between them to cup her chin in his big palm, sending a wave of goose bumps shimmering over her skin. ''Right now, you need help. Please, let me do the neighborly thing and lend a hand.''

She caught her lower lip between her teeth to keep it from trembling. Where else was she going to go? She had a newborn to take care of, no place to live and she'd exhausted her bank account to make the move from Sacramento to Wyoming. If it was just her, she'd politely refuse Morgan's offer. But she had to think of what was best for Timmy now.

''I don't have any other choice,'' she finally said,

blinking back tears. "And I really hate not having options."

"I know, sweetheart. I feel the same way." His understanding smile warmed her to the depths of her soul. "But you'll be on your feet and back in charge of things before you know it."

As she stared into his incredibly blue eyes, Samantha wondered if he'd ever been in a situation that he couldn't control. She doubted it. A man like Morgan was always in complete command of everything going on around him.

Resigned, she took a deep breath. "I'll need to get some things from my car."

He released her chin and turned his attention to the road ahead of them. Shifting the truck into drive, he nodded. "After I got back from taking you and the baby to the hospital yesterday, I had a couple of my ranch hands take one of the tractors and tow your car over here. One of them is a pretty fair mechanic and he's got it down at the machine shed, trying to get it running again."

Before Samantha could tell him to keep track of how much the repairs cost, they topped a hill overlooking a beautiful valley. A sprawling log ranch house, along with several neat-looking barns and outbuildings stood majestically at one end, while a large herd of black cattle grazed at the other.

"Is that your ranch?"

He nodded. "That's the main house. My brother,

Brant, and his wife, Annie, have their home about three miles east of here.''

"How big *is* this place?" Samantha asked incredulously.

"We've been on Lonetree land ever since we turned off the highway," he answered without blinking an eye.

"That was some time ago," she said, awed by the idea of such a large piece of property.

He nodded. "About six miles."

"Well, it certainly is beautiful," she said, marveling at the contrast between her newly inherited property and this well-kept ranch. She wondered if she'd ever be able to get hers looking as nice. If she could, she knew for certain she'd be able to find backers for the camp she wanted to open for homeless children.

Morgan didn't say anything, but she could tell by the slight curving at the corners of his mouth that her comment had pleased him.

When they drew closer, he turned the truck onto a lane that led to the house. Tall wooden posts stood on either side of the road, supporting a log spanning the width between them. As they passed beneath it, Samantha caught a fleeting glimpse of the words Lonetree Ranch carved into a wooden sign suspended from the middle of the arch.

He stopped the pickup at the side of the house, then got out and came around to help her from the passenger side. "I had Bettylou, the wife of the man working on your car, come by and make up one of the guest rooms,'' he said, unfastening the lap belt from the baby's carrier. He lifted it from the center of the bench seat, then using the handle, carried it in one hand as he cupped her elbow with the other to guide her up the steps of the front porch. ''After I get you two settled in your room, I'll go down to the machine shed and check to see if Frank knows what's wrong with your car. I'll get your things while I'm at it.''

His big hand warmed her arm through the light jacket she wore and sent a tremor up her spine. She quickly stepped away from him.

''I won't need everything from the car,'' she said, waiting for him to open the door. ''Timmy and I won't be staying more than a couple of days.''

Holding the door for her, he smiled. ''We'll see.''

She needed to make it clear to him, she wasn't a charity case, nor did she intend to take advantage of his generosity. Before she could respond to his obvious disbelief, they entered the foyer of the Lonetree ranch house and she forgot anything she'd been about to say. The interior of the log home was every bit as impressive as the exterior.

When Morgan led her into the great room, her breath caught. ''This is absolutely gorgeous.''

A huge stone fireplace with a split log mantel stood against the outside wall of the room, the rounded blue, gray and tan stones the perfect accent to the golden hue of the varnished log walls. The house had a warm, friendly feel to it, but it was the openness that Samantha fell in love with. The ceiling was vaulted and open all the way to the huge log rafters, and the rooms seemed to flow from one into another.

"Make yourself at home," Morgan said, placing the car seat with her sleeping son on the most unusual coffee table she'd ever seen.

A thick, flat piece of dark blue-gray slate rested on a pedestal base made from a section of an entire tree trunk. The bark had been left on and contrasted beautifully with the warm patina of the polished hardwood floor and the burnt sienna colored leather furniture.

"Were you going for durability?" she asked dryly.

Chuckling, Morgan shrugged. "Brant and I ruined the surface of my mom's other table so many times by running our cars and trucks over it, that Mom and Dad came up with the idea of a slate topped table before Colt was born. Then after Mom died, and Dad was faced with raising three rowdy boys by himself, I don't think he had much choice but to keep it."

"You were raised by your father?"

She noticed a fleeting shadow in his intense blue eyes a moment before he nodded. "Mom died while giving birth to our youngest brother, Colt."

Samantha gazed up at him for several long seconds. "I'm sorry, Morgan. I know what it feels like to lose your mother," she said quietly. "I was almost seventeen when mine passed away."

As they stood staring at each other, the baby suddenly let loose with a lusty cry, breaking the somber mood that had come over the two adults.

"It's time for him to nurse," she said, releasing the straps securing Timmy in the baby seat. "Is there somewhere I could—"

"I'll show you to your room," Morgan said, nodding toward the staircase behind her. The stairs, banister and railings of the loft area above were crafted from the same golden wood as the walls, and added to the rustic appeal of the house.

Samantha held the baby close and tried to concentrate on breathing as she climbed the split-log steps beside Morgan. He'd placed his arm around her waist to steady her and his touch was doing some very strange things to her insides. Tingles raced the length of her spine and a warm, protected feeling seemed to course through her.

Needing to put a little distance between them, she waited for him to lead the way across the loft and down a hall where several bedrooms were located. Her uncharacteristic reaction to him had to be due to a major postnatal hormone imbalance. That's all it could be, she decided. After giving birth two days ago, there was no way she could possibly be feeling any kind of physical awareness. Was there?

When he opened the door to a room at the end of the hall, her eyes misted over. A cradle, made up with soft-looking, baby-blue bedding sat by a beautiful four-poster bed. She couldn't remember a time since her mother's passing that anyone had been as thoughtful as Morgan had been in the past few hours. He'd made sure she and the baby had a ride home from the hospital, offered them a place to stay and had gone to the trouble of arranging for Timmy to have a warm, comfortable place to sleep.

She put her son in the cradle, then turned back to Morgan. Reaching up to place her hand at the back of his neck, she drew his head down to kiss his lean cheek. "You're the most thoughtful man I've ever met," she said, her voice shaking slightly from the emotion welling up inside of her.

Before she could draw away, Morgan pulled her into his arms, then staring down at her for no more than a split second, lowered his mouth to hers and kissed her. It wasn't anything more than his lips pressed to hers, but her knees shook and her head swam. Then, just as quickly, he released her with a muttered curse.

Looking as startled as she felt, he started backing from the room. "I...I'll get your things from the car."

Before she could remind him that she wouldn't be needing everything, he turned on his heel and left the room so fast Samantha wouldn't have been surprised to see that his boots had left skid marks on the polished hardwood floor.

She brought her fingers up to touch her tingling lips. Why had he kissed her? But more important, why did she feel like she wanted him to kiss her again?

Turning to pick up Timmy, she decided that it would definitely be in her best interest to find somewhere else to stay as soon as her car was repaired. Although Morgan Wakefield had shown her more concern and kind consideration than anyone had in longer than she cared to remember, he also represented a temptation that she wasn't ready to deal with and wasn't sure she would ever be able to resist.

Three

His jaw clenched so tightly it would probably take an oral surgeon to pry it apart, Morgan descended the stairs and crossed the great room to the front foyer. Once he stood outside on the porch, he took in several deep breaths in hopes of clearing his head. He couldn't believe what he'd just done.

Samantha had only meant that little peck on the cheek as an expression of gratitude. There hadn't been anything sexual about the gesture.

But his body hadn't seen it that way. When she'd drawn his head down to press her soft lips to his jaw, he'd responded with a fierceness that had almost knocked him to his knees. And, like a damned fool, he'd grabbed her and kissed her like a teenager with more hormones than sense.

At least he'd come to his senses before he had the chance to take the kiss to the next level. He uttered a pithy curse. So why was he regretting that he'd kept it simple?

Grinding his back teeth, he stared at the acres of pasture stretching out in front of him. Like the grass in the fields, his body was just awakening from an extended dormant period. That's all there was to it. The winter had been a long, cold one, and it was only natural that a man would be feeling the effects of not having a woman around to help him stay warm.

He ran a frustrated hand across the back of his neck and swore a blue streak. What he needed was a night in the arms of a willing woman. Then maybe he could forget how Samantha's amber eyes reminded him of long sultry nights, of tangled sheets and soft sighs.

Unfortunately, he had a feeling that it was more than the need for sexual release that caused his reaction to her. And that's what bothered him.

Since his fiancée's death, he hadn't allowed himself to look at another woman for anything more than a few hours of harmless, consensual fun. And that only happened once or twice a year when the loneliness got so bad he thought he'd jump out of his own skin.

The all too familiar ache of guilt and regret settled in his chest as he thought of Emily Swensen. They should have been celebrating their sixth wedding anniversary in a couple of months. Instead, he would be making his annual trip to the cemetery down in Denver to place flowers on her grave.

Gazing down the lane, Morgan thought about the woman he'd promised to marry. Emily had been his best friend, as well as his lover. And she'd be alive today if it wasn't for him.

He took a deep shuddering breath. He'd been so sure that he knew what was best for her when he'd insisted she make that trip to Denver to visit her sister the week before they were to be married. She hadn't wanted to go, but he'd convinced her of how lonely it would be for her while he caught up on spring chores. She'd finally agreed to make the trip, but the day she left she'd had tears running down her cheeks, as if she'd known they would never see each other again.

That was the last time he'd seen her alive. Two days later, he'd received the phone call that still haunted his dreams. Emily had been killed, and her sister seriously wounded, in the cross fire between police and a couple of thugs trying to rob a jewelry store in downtown Denver.

Guilt knotted his gut, the feeling so strong it took his breath. His presumption that he knew what was best had gotten an innocent woman killed, and proven that his judgement was faulty. He'd never run the risk of making another mistake like that again.

He'd come to terms with never having a wife and family, and he'd learned to live with the loneliness, the cold, empty spot beside him in his bed. And that's the way it was going to remain.

In a few days, he'd offer Samantha quite a bit more

for her grandfather's ranch than it was worth, insuring that she wouldn't have any money worries for a while. Then she and her son could move on, and he'd settle back down to his routine of running the Lonetree and making it the best privately owned ranch in the state of Wyoming.

"Hey, boss? You got a minute?"

Morgan turned toward the sound of Frank Milford's voice. He'd been so lost in his disturbing thoughts, he hadn't heard the man's approach.

"What do you need, Frank?" he asked, descending the porch steps.

"I think you'd better get Ned and Chico to haul that hunk of junk down at the machine shed to a scrap yard," the man said, wiping grease from his hands with a rag.

"It's that bad?" Morgan asked as he continued walking toward the shed.

"It ain't worth the powder and lead to blow it up with," Frank said, falling into step beside Morgan.

"What's wrong with it?"

"What ain't?" Frank asked disgustedly.

"You want to cut to the chase and give me a rundown so I'll know what it will take to fix it?" Morgan asked patiently. He was used to Frank's tendency to exaggerate.

Frank shook his head. "When I put a new battery in it and fired 'er up, there was a real wicked knock in the engine. Besides needin' spark plugs, new belts and hoses, I'd say it's getting ready to throw a rod."

"How long would it take to rebuild the motor?" Morgan asked, knowing it would take longer than he was comfortable with.

The sooner Samantha's car was fixed, the sooner she and her son could be on their way with a nice fat check in her pocket. Then maybe he wouldn't feel as if he were outgrowing his jeans every time she looked at him with those whiskey-brown eyes of hers.

"It'll probably take a couple of weeks," Frank said. "Maybe longer." He followed Morgan into the building they used to repair and maintain the ranching equipment. "Ford doesn't make that model anymore. Hell, I'm not even sure we can still get parts for it."

A relieved feeling swept through Morgan, quickly followed by a knot twisting at his gut. He had a feeling that Samantha would be staying a lot longer than either of them had anticipated. What bothered him was how much the idea appealed to him.

Shaking his head, he decided that a psychologist would have a field day with that one. "Go ahead and make a few calls to see what you can come up with, Frank."

"You're the boss," the man said, tossing the greasy rag onto a workbench. "But if it was me, I'd cut my losses and find another set of wheels."

As Frank walked over to the phone to start calling auto parts stores down in Laramie, Morgan opened the driver's door of Samantha's car to grab the keys from the ignition. Opening the trunk, he pulled out a couple of battered pieces of luggage, and a sack filled with what looked like baby items.

Tucking the sack under his arm, he picked up a suitcase in each hand and started for the house. Samantha wasn't going to be happy about the turn of events. For one thing, she clearly couldn't afford to have the car repaired. And for another, her stay at the Lonetree had just been extended for an indefinite period of time.

The relief he'd felt earlier increased, causing Morgan to utter a cuss word he reserved for the most serious of situations. The long, cold winter must have been longer and colder than he'd realized. He wanted a woman and baby underfoot—reminding him of the family he'd never have—about as much as he wanted to see the cattle market take a nosedive.

"Are you sure it's that serious?" Samantha asked. "When I left Sacramento, it was fine." She frowned. "Except for a clunking sound when the motor was running."

Morgan swallowed the bite of sandwich he'd been chewing and nodded. "It's not a matter of *if* the engine breaks down, it's more like *when*. It might last for another few hundred miles, or it could blow a rod before you got it backed out of the machine shed."

"I can't afford this right now." She placed her sandwich back on her plate untouched. Only moments ago, the roast beef and cheddar melt had looked delicious. But with Morgan's news about her car, Samantha's appetite deserted her.

"Don't worry about it." He took a drink of his iced tea, then shrugged. "It's taken—"

"Don't you dare," she warned.

"What?"

"You know what." She shook her head. "This is my problem and I'll solve it. You took care of the hospital bill before I could stop you. But you will *not* pay for the repairs on my car."

He gave her an exasperated look. "I've already got Frank calling auto parts stores."

"Then you can tell him to stop," she said stubbornly. "I'll just have to take my chances and hope the engine will make it until I'm able to afford to have it repaired."

"Don't be ridiculous, Samantha." His intense blue gaze caught and held hers. "What if you're out on the road with the baby and it breaks down? You can't walk miles for help with an infant, nor can you wait for someone to come along and find you." He shook his head. "This isn't a highly populated area. Out here, there are times when it's hours before another car comes by."

Her heart sank. Morgan was right. She couldn't run the risk of being out with Timmy in an unreliable car.

She took a deep breath and had to force herself to admit defeat. "All right. Have the car repaired. But only on one condition." When he cocked a dark brow, she added, "You have to let me know every penny you spend on it, so that I can reimburse you."

"I'm not worried about—"

"I am," she interrupted. She had to make him understand. "After my father left us without a backward glance, I watched my mother struggle to keep a roof over our heads and food in our mouths. It wasn't easy for her, but she did it without waiting for a man to come to the rescue. I fully intend to do the same." Rising from the table, she wrapped her sandwich and placed it in the refrigerator. "I don't ever intend to rely on anyone for what I want or need. I'll work for it and earn it, or I'll do without."

He looked as if he were about to protest, but Samantha held up her hand to stop him. "I know you mean well, but this is something I feel very strongly about. It's no secret, I've hit a low spot in my life. But it's only temporary. As soon as the doctor releases me to work, I'll get a job and pay you back." She started to leave the kitchen, but a sudden thought had her turning back. "Do you have a housekeeper or cook?"

In the middle of taking a long swig of his iced tca, he slowly placed the glass on the table and shook his head. "No. I usually take my meals down at the bunkhouse with the rest of the guys. And when I need something done to the house, my sister-in-law, Annie, takes care of it, or I pay Bettylou. Why?"

Samantha nodded. "Until my car is repaired and I find a job to pay you back, you won't be needing their help. I'll be cooking your meals and cleaning your house.''

Morgan's eyes narrowed as he watched her turn and slowly walk from the room, shoulders straight, her head held high. He'd always admired those who had the grit to work and make their own way. But Samantha was taking this pride thing to the extreme. He could tell by the way she moved that she was still sore from giving birth, yet she was telling him that she was going to start cooking and cleaning for him?

''Like hell,'' he muttered.

Scooting his chair back from the table, he rinsed his plate and glass, then placed them in the dishwasher and headed for his study. He had the perfect solution to resolve the money issue that she seemed to think was so important.

She owned the run-down ranch that he wanted to buy. What could be more simple than him offering to buy it from her? He would end up with the land he wanted, and she'd have the cash to get on her feet and start a new, more secure life for herself and her son.

Morgan ignored the twinge in his gut at the thought of Samantha leaving as he dialed his attorney and made arrangements for the man to draw up a purchase option. Assured that the document would be delivered within the next week or two, he climbed the stairs and walked down the hall to Samantha's door. The sound of the baby crying immediately caught his attention.

"Samantha?" he called, tapping on the door.

Nothing.

Opening it a crack, he tried again. "Samantha, I'd like to talk to you—"

The sound of the shower running explained why she wasn't tending to the baby. He glanced from the closed door of the adjoining bathroom to the cradle where Timmy continued to wail at the top of his little lungs. Now what? Samantha was taking a shower and Timmy sounded as if he was gearing up for a real rip-snorter of a fit.

Morgan walked over to the tiny bed to rock it back and forth, hoping to quiet the baby until Samantha finished her shower. "Shhh, little guy. Your mom will be here in just a minute."

If anything the baby cried harder.

Deciding he didn't have a choice, Morgan held his breath and gingerly picked up the infant. The only other times in his life that he'd held a baby had been when he'd helped Samantha give birth, then just a few hours ago when he'd brought her and Timmy home from the hospital. Now what was he supposed to do?

"They should issue 'how-to' manuals on this stuff," he muttered, feeling like a fish out of water.

He mentally reviewed how he'd seen Samantha hold little Timmy when he'd started crying earlier. The baby seemed to be quiet whenever she held him to her shoulder. Maybe that was his favorite position.

Morgan put the infant to his shoulder and rubbed

the little guy's back like he'd seen Samantha do. Timmy instantly stopped crying and let loose with a burp that Morgan was sure rattled his tiny rib cage.

He couldn't help it, Morgan laughed out loud. "I'll bet you feel better now, don't you?" He felt something wet seep through his shirt, and glancing at his shoulder, cringed. "I guess you had a little too much for lunch, huh?"

"What's wrong?" Samantha asked as she came out of the bathroom and hurried over to him. She took the baby, then gasped. "Oh, my. Your shirt." She placed the now quiet baby back in the cradle and grabbed a box of moist towelettes from the dresser. "I'm so sorry."

Morgan swallowed hard and shifted from one foot to the other as Samantha leaned close to wipe the spot from his shirt. Her nearness was doing a hell of a number on his insides. She smelled like lilacs and sweet woman, and her warm breath whispering over the exposed skin at the open vee of his shirt had his heart pounding so hard, he figured she could feel it beneath her fingers.

As he stared down at her, he took note of several things. Her hair was wrapped in a towel on top of her head, exposing the delicate skin of her slender neck. The long thick lashes framing her pretty eyes looked all dewy from her shower.

But the most noticeable, and most disturbing thing about her, was the way the top of her fluffy yellow robe gapped open. It gave him more than a fair view of the slope of her breasts, and the realization that she probably didn't have a stitch on beneath that robe sent blood rushing through his veins and made his jeans feel like they were way too short in the stride.

Quickly backing away from her before he did something stupid, like grab her and kiss her again, he headed for the door. "When you have time, I'd like to talk to you downstairs," he said as he stepped out into the hall. He quickly reached back to pull the door shut. "I'll be in my office."

Samantha stared at the closed door for several long seconds before she finally released the breath she hadn't been aware of holding. The earthy scents of leather, sunshine and virile male had her pulse racing and goose bumps skipping over her skin.

But it had been the feel of Morgan's pectoral muscles beneath her fingers that made her knees feel rubbery and had her catching her breath. The man was built as solid as a rock and she wondered how it would feel to be held against all that sinew, to be wrapped in arms so strong they could easily crush her, yet were gentle enough to hold a baby.

"Stop it," she chided herself.

She plopped the box of baby wipes back on the dresser, then reached up to jerk the towel from her wet hair. Her crazy postnatal hormones had to be the reason for her uncharacteristic behavior. That's all it could be. She wasn't interested in Morgan Wakefield or any other man.

Satisfied that she'd discovered the reason for her strong reaction to him, she dried her hair and traded her robe for a pink cotton, dropped-waist dress that buttoned up the front. Checking on Timmy, sleeping peacefully in the cradle, she turned on one of the baby monitors Morgan had brought in from the trunk of her car, then picking up the listening unit, walked out into the hall.

As she descended the stairs, she wondered what Morgan could possibly want to discuss with her. She'd made it quite clear that she intended to earn her and Timmy's keep while they stayed here, and if he thought he was going to talk her out of it, he had another think coming.

Determined to set Mr. Morgan Wakefield straight, she crossed the great room and front foyer to tap on the frame of the open office door. He held a cordless phone to his ear with one shoulder as he shuffled through several papers lying on top of his desk.

"Is this a bad time?" she whispered.

Shaking his head, he motioned for her to enter the room and sit in one of the two comfortable-looking leather armchairs in front of the shiny walnut desk. "I'll check the breeding records for those two mares and get back with you on that, Brant." Morgan ended the call, then smiling, turned his attention to her. "I think I've come up with a solution to your money worries."

She settled back in one of the chairs across from him and tried not to think about how attractive he looked. Morgan had the nicest smile, and she had a feeling if he set his mind to it, he could charm the birds out of the trees. Fortunately for her, she didn't have feathers.

"You've found a job for me, other than cooking and cleaning?" she asked carefully.

His grin widened as he shook his head. "No."

His gaze held hers, causing her heart to skip a beat and making her feel like a night creature caught in the headlights of an oncoming car. She glanced to the bookshelves beyond his shoulder in order to keep from drowning in the depths of his intense blue eyes.

"What do you have in mind, if it's not a job?"

"Since discovering that your grandfather's place isn't in any shape for you to take up residence, you could sell the land," he said, making it sound extremely simple.

Smiling, she shook her head. "No. That's not an option."

His grin faded and he looked as if it had been the last thing he expected her to say. "Why not?"

"I have plans for that property."

"You do?" He looked extremely interested in what she had planned. It made her feel a little more confident.

Samantha glanced down at her hands resting in her lap as she tried to put her dream into words. "I never got to meet my grandfather because he and my mother didn't get along. He didn't approve of her choice of men, and my mother was too stubborn to admit that he'd been right about my father. To my knowledge he never even knew about me, any more than I knew that he existed." Taking a deep breath to chase away the sadness she always felt when she thought of her father, she raised her gaze to meet Morgan's. "When Daddy left us, my mother refused to come back here and admit that she'd made a mistake. Now she's gone, I haven't seen my father since I was four years old, and I have no brothers or sisters. I know it doesn't make a lot of sense, but that property is all I have that ties me to any kind of family and makes me feel like I belong."

The last thing Morgan expected was for Samantha to have any kind of sentimental attachment to a place that she hadn't even known existed until a few weeks ago. But what was even more baffling about it was that he understood how she felt. The Lonetree was as much a part of him as the blood running through his veins.

"Are you going to try to fix up the house?" he finally managed to ask. He knew full well that she didn't have the funds to do much more than tack a piece of plastic over the holes in the roof.

Nodding, her eyes lit with enthusiasm. "I not only intend to live there, I'm going to open a summer retreat for homeless and abandoned children. I know it will take a while to get things the way I'd like, and I'll probably have to get a job to support myself while I look for financial help to get the camp started, but I'm hoping to have it ready to open next year."

"What kind of job did you have before you left California?" he asked, already anticipating her answer.

"I was a social worker for the county until government cutbacks forced the elimination of several jobs, including mine. It was my responsibility to place abandoned and orphaned children, either with relatives or in foster care." Her pretty face softened as she explained, and Morgan could tell this was something very close to her heart. "I want to continue helping children, who, for whatever reason, find themselves separated from their families. I want to make a place where they can forget, if only for a week or two, the reasons they aren't with their parents."

Morgan didn't know what to say. Her reasons for wanting to hang on to the place were a hell of a lot more noble than what he wanted to do with the property. Helping kids beat raising bucking horses for the rodeo circuit, hands down. He suddenly felt guilty as hell at even suggesting she sell the property.

"Were you put into foster care after your mother died?" he asked, beginning to understand her desire to help children she didn't know.

He watched sadness fill her eyes as she nodded. "When my mother died, I was just like these children. I suddenly found that I no longer had a place where I belonged."

The thought that she'd been alone at such a young age with no one to turn to, tied his stomach in knots. He'd had his brothers when they lost their dad. But

Samantha had been completely alone. He had to fight the urge to round the desk and take her into his arms.

"Were you placed with a good family?" he asked, needing to know that she'd had someone to take care of her.

To his relief, she nodded. "Since I was almost seventeen, I wasn't in the system much over a year. I was fortunate enough to be taken in by a very kind, older couple. They treated me like a granddaughter and I will always be grateful for that. But some children aren't as lucky as I was. Some are taken care of, but not cared for. There's a difference."

"What will you do until you get the camp started?" he asked, mentally reviewing who he knew in county government who might be able to help her get on as a case worker with social services.

"Now that I have Timmy, I'd like to find something that I could do at home, or only be away from him a minimal amount of time."

Morgan could understand her desire to be with the baby. He didn't like the idea of her being away from the little guy either.

His heart slammed into his rib cage. Where had that come from? Why should he care? Timmy wasn't his child.

But whether the baby belonged to him or not, Morgan felt a responsibility toward Samantha and her little boy that defied logic or reason. And it scared him spitless.

Between the sudden urge to help her find a way to

keep the ranch he'd wanted to buy for as long as he could remember, and the protective feelings that were building inside of him at an alarming rate, Morgan suddenly felt as if he couldn't breathe.

Rising from his chair, he grabbed his Resistol, jammed it on his head and rounded the desk. "I…uh, just remembered something I need to do," he said, knowing his excuse sounded as lame as it was. "If you want me for anything, call Frank down at the machine shed. He'll know where to find me."

She rose to follow him. "Do you mind if I look around the kitchen to see what I can make for dinner?"

He turned back to stare at her. She looked so damned pretty standing there gazing up at him that it took every ounce of willpower he possessed to keep from pulling her to him.

Slowly shaking his head, he warned, "Just don't overdo things. You got that?"

She gave him a smile that just about knocked his boots off. "Will do, boss."

"I'm not—" he took a step forward and reached out to cup her soft cheek in his palm "—your boss, sweetheart."

Her easy expression turned into one of awareness, then staunch determination. "You are until Timmy and I leave here."

He shook his head. "No—" he leaned forward to brush his lips over hers "—I'm not."

Turning, he walked from the room, out the front

door and headed for the barn. If he hadn't walked away when he did, he'd have ended up taking her into his arms and kissing her until they both needed CPR.

As he entered the barn he decided checking the fence in the north pasture wasn't a bad idea. He could ride for hours with nothing more to do than try to figure out what the hell had gotten into him, and what he had to do to keep from getting in deeper than he already was.

Saddling his favorite gelding, he led the sorrel out of the barn, then swung up into the saddle. It didn't make a damned bit of sense. He'd only known Samantha for three days.

But with each passing minute, the need to help her and her tiny son became stronger. And every time he looked into her pretty amber eyes, it sure as hell felt like he was about to drown.

Four

After Morgan left, it took Samantha several minutes to bring her pulse back under control. What in the name of heaven was wrong with her? She wasn't interested in Morgan Wakefield or any other man. Between her father and Chad, she'd learned a valuable lesson. Men couldn't be counted on for anything, and only ended up letting a woman down in one way or another.

She'd had quite enough of that, thank you very much. She certainly didn't need to set herself up for more.

The best way to avoid being disappointed by a man was not to become involved with one to begin with. Period. As long as she kept that in mind, she'd be just fine.

With a determined nod, she headed for the kitchen. She'd told Morgan that she intended to cook and clean for him to pay for her and Timmy's keep. Until she gained her full strength back, she'd have to watch what she did. But as long as she didn't do anything too strenuous, and took frequent breaks, the activity would be good for her.

Setting the baby monitor on the counter, she found some paper and a pen to jot down things she'd need from the store, and started taking inventory of what Morgan had on hand. Two hours later, her grocery list filled three full sheets of paper and had her shaking her head. Besides some packages of beef in the freezer, there really wasn't a whole lot to work with.

"Samantha?"

At the unexpected sound of the female voice calling her name, Samantha jumped. Walking out of the pantry, she watched a petite blond-haired woman use the heel of her boot to shut the back door behind her, then hurry over to set two paper grocery bags on the counter.

When the woman turned to face Samantha, her smile was warm and friendly. "I'm Annie Wakefield. I'm married to Morgan's brother, Brant."

"It's nice to meet you, Annie." She smiled and motioned to the list she held. "I was just taking stock of what I could make for dinner."

Annie laughed. "I'm afraid the Wakefield men are rather limited when it comes to their diet. If it didn't moo before it went to the packing house, they don't eat it.''

"I've noticed," Samantha said, grinning. "I've found several steaks and a couple of roasts in the freezer, but that's about it.''

"That's why I brought over a few staples," Annie said, motioning to the bags on the counter. "While he was out riding fence, Morgan stopped by our place and mentioned that he had a guest. I know from past experience how empty that pantry is, so I gathered some things and headed this way.''

Samantha nodded. "I was beginning to wonder what I was going to do with frozen beef, half a loaf of stale bread and a jar of grape jelly.''

Annie frowned as she pulled items from the two sacks. "It's worse than usual. What did you have for dinner?''

Confused, Samantha shook her head. "We haven't had dinner yet.''

"I meant lunch." Annie grinned. "The first thing I learned when I married Brant was that dinner is the noon meal, supper is the evening meal and the word lunch isn't part of the Wakefield vocabulary.''

"I'll have to remember that," Samantha said, liking Annie Wakefield more with each passing second. "Morgan had one of the men bring a couple of sandwiches up from the bunkhouse for lun…I mean dinner, but—''

"Don't tell me he fed you one of Leon's roast beef

and cheddar melts,'' Annie interrupted. She made a face. ''They're horrible.''

Samantha shook her head. ''I lost my appetite after learning my car is in need of major work. I put my sandwich in the refrigerator.''

''Believe me, you don't want to go there.'' Wrinkling her nose, Annie opened the refrigerator door, plucked the wrapped sandwich from the shelf and tossed it in the trash. She placed a half gallon of milk, a tub of margarine and a package of cheese inside, then closed the door. ''Leon means well, but he thinks everything he makes has to be smothered in hot sauce and horseradish.''

Samantha shuddered at the thought of the indigestion she and Timmy would both have suffered from all that spice. ''I'm glad I didn't try it. It wouldn't have been good for my baby.''

Annie gave her an understanding smile. ''Morgan told us what happened. Are you both doing all right? Is there anything I can do to help?''

The woman's compassion touched Samantha deeply. Before coming to Wyoming, she couldn't remember the last time anyone cared if she was all right, or if she needed help.

''We're fine,'' she said, blinking back tears. She'd no sooner gotten the words out than Timmy's lusty cry came through the speaker of the baby monitor. Laughing shakily, she added, ''Well, we will be as soon as he nurses.''

"Then you'd better not keep him waiting," Annie said, smiling back at her.

"I'll be back down as soon as he's finished," Samantha said, picking up the monitoring unit. "Thank you for being so thoughtful. I truly appreciate it."

"I have to admit to having an ulterior motive," Annie said, smiling. "I want to spend some time around your baby to see what I'm getting myself into."

"You're pregnant?"

When she nodded, Annie looked absolutely radiant. "I used one of the early home tests this morning."

"That's wonderful," Samantha said, reaching out to hug her new friend. She grinned. "When I come back downstairs, I'll bring Timmy so you get the full treatment."

"That buckskin and the bay stud would throw a nice colt," Morgan said, pointing across the feed lot to the mare chewing on a mouthful of grain.

His brother, Brant, nodded. "That's what I've been thinking. With those bloodlines, it should buck hard enough to rattle a few brains, too."

Morgan grinned. "Speaking of rattled brains, how did our little brother do this past weekend in Grand Rapids?"

"Colt rode all three of his bulls, but Mitch Simpson won the event," Brant answered. A rodeo bullfighter, Brant worked most of the Professional Bull Riders events that their younger brother competed in. "Colt ended up with a nice hefty check for his efforts, though.''

''Good. Maybe he'll pay me the fifty bucks he owes me,'' Morgan said, turning to walk toward the house.

''What did you two bet on this time?'' Brant asked, falling into step beside Morgan.

''Baseball. He said the Rockies would sweep the four-game series against the Cardinals. I said they wouldn't.'' Morgan grinned. ''He didn't know that the Cardinals took their star pitcher off the disabled list last week. I did.''

Brant laughed. ''Well, you'll have to wait a couple of weeks for him to pay up. Colt went home with Mitch this weekend to help put up a fence.''

''Every time we stretch fence around here, he's as scarce as hen's teeth,'' Morgan said, frowning.

He could understand his youngest brother's desire to help his best friend. Since Mitch and his sister Kaylee lost their parents in a car accident three years ago, Mitch had his hands full keeping the family ranch going, as well as competing at the top level of the Professional Bull Riders organization. But Colt needed to remember there was work to be done around the Lonetree, too.

''The scenery is nicer on Mitch's ranch than it is here,'' Brant said, his grin meaningful.

''Kaylee?'' When Brant nodded, Morgan shook his head. ''How long do you think it will take before the two of them wake up and smell the coffee?''

Brant shrugged. "Who knows? You know how stubborn our baby brother is."

Morgan laughed as they walked across the yard. "About as stubborn as you were when you met Annie."

"Hey, I finally came to my senses and saw the light." His smile fading, Brant asked, "Do you think Tug's granddaughter is really serious about starting a camp for foster kids? Or do you think she'll eventually give up and sell out?"

Morgan shook his head. "I don't know. She doesn't really have the money to do anything, but she's determined enough not to let that stop her."

"You know, we don't really need the land," Brant said thoughtfully.

"Nope." Morgan shrugged. "It would be nice not to have that two hundred acre chunk out of the middle of the Lonetree's western boundary, but it's been that way for the last seventy-five years."

Brant grinned. "So what's another seventy-five? Right?"

"Right," Morgan agreed, returning his brother's easy expression.

As soon as they entered the house, the unfamiliar sight of two women working side by side in his kitchen stopped Morgan short. He was used to seeing his sister-in-law, Annie, make an occasional meal for all of them during calving season or fall roundup. But seeing Samantha with a smear of flour on her chin and her cheeks flushed from the heat of the oven, reminded Morgan of everything he'd wanted, but never hoped to have—a wife, a family and a home filled with love and laughter.

He watched Brant walk up behind Annie, wrap his arms around her waist and kiss her like a soldier returning from war. Remembering the feel of Samantha's soft lips beneath his, Morgan swallowed hard. Why was he having to fight the urge to keep from doing the same thing to her?

Hells bells, what was wrong with him? He really didn't even know the woman.

As he watched Annie laughingly introduce Brant to Samantha, Morgan mentally calculated when he could take time off from the ranch for a drive down to Bear Creek. No doubt about it. He needed to make that trip to Buffalo Gals for a night of good old-fashioned hell-raising. And damned quick. Otherwise, he was going to be as crazy as a loon and climbing the walls by the end of the week.

The baby, sitting in his carrier on top of the table, suddenly let loose with a wail, gaining everyone's attention.

"He probably needs burping again," Samantha said, grabbing a towel to wipe her hands.

"I'll take care of it," Morgan said, clearly surprising Annie and Brant. He ignored their questioning looks as he gazed down at the baby. "You and I have a little experience in this area, don't we?"

Samantha grinned. "Don't forget to place the end of the receiving blanket over your shoulder."

He couldn't help it, he grinned right back. "Good idea. I've only got a couple of clean shirts left." He ignored his brother's gaping expression, carefully lifted Timmy from the carrier and held him to his shoulder. "Come on, little guy. We'll walk around a little and see if that helps." Turning back to Samantha, he warned, "Don't overdo things. If you get tired, sit down and put your feet up."

Morgan caught the questioning looks exchanged between Brant and Annie, and he wasn't a bit surprised when his brother followed him down the hall to the great room.

"Uh, bro, you want to let me in on what's going on?" Brant asked, his smile irritating enough to make Morgan want to bite nails in two.

"There's nothing going on," Morgan answered as he gently patted Timmy's back. "Samantha and Annie are both busy, and the baby needs a little attention. I'm just helping out."

Brant snorted. "Yeah, right. To my knowledge, you've never held a baby before in your life." He pointed to Timmy. "But you sure as hell look like you know what you're doing with this one."

"If you'll remember, I had a crash course in babies a few nights ago," Morgan said, continuing to rub the baby's tiny back. When Timmy burped loudly, Morgan chuckled. "That feels better, doesn't it?"

Brant shook his head in obvious wonderment. "How did you know what to do?"

"I didn't." Morgan transferred the now content

baby to the cradle of his arm. "But earlier this afternoon Samantha was busy and…" He stopped to eye his brother suspiciously. "Would *you* like to tell me why you're so interested?"

Brant hesitated before shaking his head. "Just curious."

Morgan wasn't buying it for a minute. Brant looked like the cat that swallowed the canary. "Is Annie—"

"In due time, big brother," Brant said, turning to walk back into the kitchen. "In due time."

Watching Brant saunter from the room, Morgan figured he knew what his brother was trying to keep from saying—probably under threat of bodily harm from Annie. Morgan grinned. Unless he missed his guess, he was going to be an uncle around the first part of next year, and Annie had plans of making the grand announcement during supper.

Happiness for his brother and sister-in-law filled him, followed quickly by a shaft of deep longing. Morgan had always wanted a family, but he'd have to be content with being the favorite uncle. His thinking that he knew what was best for those he cared for had already cost one life, and he couldn't take the chance of making a wrong decision for anyone else.

He gazed down at the baby in his arms. Raising a child and all the decisions it entailed was an awesome responsibility, and one that he wasn't sure he'd ever trust himself to take on. What if his judgement proved faulty a second time?

No. He never wanted to take that chance again. If

he did and something happened, he'd never be able to live with himself.

"Morgan, is everything all right?" Samantha asked as she walked into the room.

"Couldn't be better," he lied.

"You look rather…grim," she said, placing her hand on his.

A jolt of electric current immediately streaked up his arm at the contact, and he suddenly felt the need to run like hell. The mother of the baby he held was far more temptation than anything he'd had to deal with in the past six years. She was soft, sensual and represented everything he couldn't trust himself to have.

"Here," he said, handing Timmy to her. "I'll be in for supper in a few minutes. I have…a couple of things I need to do before we eat."

Knowing she was staring at him like he'd grown another head, he turned and walked straight to his office. Once inside, he closed the door and walked over to stare out the window at the shadows of evening creeping over the mountains in the distance.

He wasn't at all comfortable with his attraction to Samantha Peterson. But until her car was repaired, he'd be seeing her every time he turned around.

As he watched the cattle grazing in the distance, he came to a decision. There was enough work to do around the Lonetree each day to keep him busy from daylight until well past dark. Until Samantha's car was fixed, and she and her tiny son moved on, he'd work until he dropped if need be. But he was going to keep his distance and contact with her to a bare minimum.

He had to. It was the only way he had a prayer of a chance of keeping what little scrap of sanity he had left.

"I really enjoyed the evening," Samantha said as Annie and Brant prepared to leave.

Annie hugged her. "I did, too. Remember, if you need anything at all, don't hesitate to give me a call." She stepped back and grinned. "And especially if you need someone to baby-sit Timmy."

"I'll do that," Samantha said, smiling.

After Annie's announcement at dinner that she and Brant were expecting, the couple spent the rest of the evening asking questions about pregnancy, birth and the care of an infant. Morgan had remained extremely quiet during the conversation, but not knowing him well, Samantha wasn't sure if that was unusual or not.

"I'll bring that bay stud over tomorrow to meet his new girlfriend," Brant said, putting his arm around Annie as they walked to the door.

"I'm sure Stormy Gal will be happy to see him," Morgan answered, displaying the first genuine smile Samantha had seen from him since before dinner.

Once Brant and Annie left, Samantha returned to the great room to straighten up before she took Timmy upstairs. Now that she and Morgan were alone, she felt a bit awkward. The situation seemed so…domestic.

"I enjoyed meeting your brother and sister-in-law," she said as she straightened the colorful Native American blanket on the back of the leather couch. "You have a very nice family."

"Annie's always nice," Morgan said, walking over to the fireplace to bank the fire. When he turned back to face her, he grinned. "And Brant was on his best behavior."

Samantha could tell that Morgan was very close to his family, and she had to fight the wave of envy threatening to swamp her. She'd always wanted a brother or sister—someone to be close to, someone she could share memories with.

"I'm pretty tired," she said, suddenly feeling more alone than she'd ever felt in her entire life. Being around the Wakefields reminded her of everything she'd never had—siblings who loved and cared for her. "I think Timmy and I are going to turn in now."

Making sure the baby was securely strapped in, she started to take hold of the carrier, but Morgan was suddenly at her side, his big hand wrapping around the handle. "I don't think you should be lifting this thing just yet," he said, gruffly. "It's pretty heavy, even without the baby in it, and you've overdone things today."

"Not really." Her protest would have been a lot more effective if she hadn't had to hide a huge yawn behind her hand.

"Yeah, sure," he said, easily lifting the carrier in one hand as he placed his other hand at the small of her back. "And a donkey can fly."

"You know, I think I saw one soaring over the barn when we arrived today," she said, laughing nervously. The warmth where his hand touched her back was doing strange things to her insides.

He shook his head as he guided her to the stairs. "Nice try, but I'm not buying it. You were on your feet more than you should have been today."

"Oh, really? The other night you told me you weren't a doctor."

As soon as the words were out, she felt her cheeks heat with embarrassment. Her reference to the night Timmy was born reminded her of what had taken place and that Morgan had seen most of her secrets.

But that wasn't the issue here. She wasn't about to admit that he was probably right—that she had come close to overdoing things her first day out of the hospital. "Did you receive a medical degree in the past two days that I'm not aware of?"

"Nope. But I read the rest of that book."

Her cheeks got warmer. "When?"

"After you fell asleep the night Timmy was born," he said, opening the door to her room. He waited for her to walk in ahead of him before following her. Placing the baby carrier in the middle of the double bed, he turned to leave. "Just remember to take it easier tomorrow than you did today."

Reaching out to stop him, she placed her hand on his shoulder. "Morgan?"

She needed to thank him for all that he'd done for her and the baby in the past few days. She'd told him that he was thoughtful, but she hadn't really expressed her appreciation.

When he faced her, she started to tell him how much his generosity meant to her, but the look in his incredible blue eyes took her breath. If she didn't know better, she'd think it was desire. But that was ridiculous, she thought a moment before he reached out to pull her to him.

"Samantha," was all he said as he brought his hands up to thread his fingers through her shoulder-length hair.

Fascinated by the sound of his deep baritone saying her name, she watched him slowly lower his head. Her eyes drifted shut the second their mouths met and she brought her hands up to his chest to brace herself.

Unlike this afternoon when he'd lightly brushed her lips with his, he fused their mouths together in a kiss that seared her all the way to her very soul. He traced the seam of her mouth with his tongue, asking for her acceptance, seeking her permission to explore the sensitive recesses within.

Without a thought of denying him what he sought, she parted her lips and he slipped inside to tease and taste, to explore and entice. He moved his hands to her waist to draw her more fully against him, and Samantha felt as if his big body surrounded hers.

Without a thought to the insanity that seemed to have them both in its grip, she found herself leaning into his strength, melting against the solid wall of his chest.

But as his tongue stroked and encouraged her to reciprocate in kind, the sound of her son awakening to nurse helped to lift the sensual fog enveloping them.

Morgan was the first to move. Lifting his mouth from hers, he quickly stepped back to gaze down at her, his frown formidable. "Dammit, Samantha, I didn't mean for that to happen. I'm sorry."

Doing her best to gather her scattered thoughts, she straightened her shoulders and said the first thing that came to mind. "I'm not."

Dear heavens, what had gotten into her? Had she really said that?

"I mean…that is…"

Her cheeks felt as if they were on fire. What could she say after a blunt admission like that?

But what was more disconcerting than her outspokenness was the fact that she'd really meant it. She wasn't sorry. And that bothered her more than anything else.

His expression softened ever so slightly. "It doesn't matter, Samantha. I'm a thirty-four-year-old man, not a teenage boy with little or no control." He lifted his hand as if he intended to touch her cheek, then quickly dropped it to his side. "Starting tomorrow, you probably won't see me around much. Spring is one of the busiest times of the year on a ranch and there are a lot of things that need my attention. If you want or need something, call the barn or the machine shed and one of my men will see that I get the message.''

Then, without a backward glance, he turned and walked from the room.

Samantha stared at the closed door. Why did she suddenly feel like she'd been abandoned again? And why on earth did the knowledge that Morgan Wakefield clearly didn't want anything to do with her make her feel like she was about to break down and cry?

She shook her head and tried to dispel the all too familiar feeling. She was used to men abandoning her. At the tender age of four, her father had found another woman and walked out on her and her mother as if they'd never mattered to him. Then years later, when social services contacted him after her mother's death, he'd turned his back on her again and refused to take her in.

Picking up Timmy, she sniffed back her tears. But the most devastating abandonment of all had been Chad's response to the knowledge that he was going to be a father. It was one thing for him to cast her aside, but it was an entirely different matter for him to reject their child.

But that didn't explain her reaction to Morgan's dismissal of her. They barely knew each other, and besides, she wasn't interested in him or any other man. Men weren't reliable and couldn't be counted on to be there for a woman when she needed them most.

"These feelings I'm having for Morgan have got to be hormonal," she said aloud. Turning to pick up Timmy, she shook her head. "I'll be glad when this dumb postnatal stuff is over with and I get back on track."

Five

As Morgan left the barn and slowly walked toward the house, he stared up at the starless night sky. Every night for the past month, he'd waited until Samantha had gone to bed before calling it a day. And every morning he'd hauled his sorry butt out of bed and left the house before she came downstairs. He had seen her a few times, but with the exception of Sunday dinners and a handful of visits from Brant and Annie, he'd managed to keep his distance.

But instead of lessening the itch that started the minute he first laid eyes on her, it only seemed to aggravate it. He shook his head at his foolishness. He'd even abandoned the idea of driving down to Buffalo Gals to find a willing little filly for a night of fun and games. Something told him that he'd only end up feeling like he'd betrayed Samantha. Which was completely ridiculous. Hell, they barely knew each other.

"You're seriously screwed up, Wakefield," he muttered as he climbed the back porch steps.

Opening the door, he walked into the dimly lit kitchen and stopped short. Samantha had left the light on over the sink for him, as she always did. But instead of being upstairs in bed, she sat at the table with plans for her camp spread out, and her head pillowed on her folded arms. She was sound asleep.

He swallowed hard. She looked so damned sweet it was all he could do to keep from walking over and gathering her to him. Instead, he squatted down beside her chair to gently touch her shoulder.

"Samantha?"

"Mmm."

"Don't you think it would be more comfortable sleeping upstairs in bed?"

Her long, dark lashes fluttered a moment before she opened her eyes. The slumberous look of her amber gaze sent a shaft of longing right to his core.

He swallowed hard. This was how she'd look waking up beside him after a night of—

"I was waiting for you," she said, sitting up. She pushed her golden-brown hair back. "I need to talk to you about something."

Glancing at his watch, guilt twisted his gut that he'd kept her waiting. She'd have to get up early with the baby tomorrow morning and it was almost midnight now.

"What did you need?" he asked, using his index finger to brush a strand of hair from her porcelain cheek.

"Frank said they've back-ordered that part for my car again," she said, her voice flowing over him like a piece of soft velvet. "And I need to drive down to Laramie in the morning." She looked uncertain. "I wouldn't ask unless it was really important, but would you mind if I borrowed one of your trucks?"

Her expression told him that something was up, and that it had her worried. "Is something wrong? Do you or Timmy need to see a doctor?"

"No. We're both fine. Annie drove us to the clinic for our postnatal checkups a couple of days ago," she said, shaking her head. "But my grandfather's lawyer called this afternoon. He said there's a problem with my inheritance and he needs to meet with me."

"Did he say what was wrong?" Morgan asked, hoping for her sake there wasn't a lien, or someone claiming the property for unpaid taxes.

"I asked, but all he would say was he needed to speak with me in person so he could explain the new terms of the will." She frowned. "He didn't mention anything about there being any kind of stipulations on my inheritance when he first contacted me, or when I called five weeks ago to tell him that he could reach me here at the Lonetree."

Morgan wasn't sure what the lawyer had found, but

he didn't like the sound of it. After old Tug had died, he'd contacted the law firm about buying the property and they'd assured him the place was free and clear, should the heir wish to sell.

"I have to make the drive down to Laramie some-time this week for fencing supplies," Morgan said, thinking aloud. "I could make arrangements to go tomorrow and take you with me. Did the lawyer give you a time to be there?"

"He said any time tomorrow morning would be fine," she answered, yawning.

"What time will Timmy wake up?" Morgan asked, rising to his feet.

She yawned again. "Early."

A warm, protective feeling that he didn't care to dwell on swept over him as he gazed down at her. "Do you think you and Timmy can be ready to leave by eight tomorrow morning?"

When she nodded, he helped her gather her camp plans, then took her hand and led her toward the stairs. At the bottom step, he kissed her forehead. "Go on upstairs and get some sleep, sweetheart. We'll deal with this in the morning."

"I don't know how long I'll be," Samantha said, staring out the windshield of Morgan's truck at the entrance to the brick building housing the law firm of Greeley, Hartwell and Buford.

"Don't worry about it," Morgan said, killing the engine and releasing his seat belt. "Timmy and I will hold down things out here, while you go in and see what the 'suit' has to say."

Samantha nodded, took a deep breath and opened the passenger door. "Keep your fingers crossed that this is something minor."

"Good luck," he said, smiling as he rested his outstretched arm along the back of the bench seat.

It was easy for Morgan to look relaxed. He wasn't the one who'd talked to Mr. Greeley yesterday. The man had been extremely evasive when she asked him if he could tell her what the terms were over the phone. He'd mumbled some kind of legalese that she assumed explained why they'd need to meet in person, and she'd finally agreed. But she didn't have a good feeling about this. Not at all.

After she spoke with the receptionist, she'd barely settled into one of the uncomfortable chairs in the waiting area than a man appeared at the open door of the hallway leading toward the back of the building. "Are you Ms. Peterson?"

"Yes."

When she rose to her feet, the balding little man gave her a nervous smile. "I'm Gerald Greeley," he said, extending his hand. "If you'll come on back to my office, I'll explain the mix-up."

Samantha's stomach suddenly felt queasy as she shook his hand and followed him down the hall. Something told her this wasn't going to be something simple, nor was he going to tell her anything she'd want to hear.

As they entered a small, nondescript office, he motioned to a chair across from his desk. "Please have a seat."

"What's this all about, Mr. Greeley?" she asked, perching on the edge of the seat. "I thought everything was in order."

"So did we." He sighed heavily and sank into the executive chair behind the desk. "But there was a wrinkle that cropped up yesterday morning we couldn't have anticipated."

She eyed him carefully. Sweat had popped out on his forehead and he looked as if he dreaded what he had to say next.

"Why don't you just tell me and get it over with?" she asked, feeling more apprehensive by the second.

"You haven't by any chance gotten married in the past month, have you, Ms. Peterson?" the man asked, sounding hopeful.

She eyed him suspiciously. "No. Why do you ask?"

"Because to claim the land your grandfather bequeathed you, you'll have to be married, and remain that way for the next two years," he said, digging a white linen handkerchief from the inside pocket of his suit coat to wipe the sweat from his brow.

In a daze, Samantha spent the next half hour listening as Gerald Greeley explained the terms of the new will, and why the law firm had been unaware of its existence. By the time she walked out of the office and back to Morgan's truck, her stomach churned unmercifully and she felt a good cry coming on.

When Samantha opened the truck door and got in, Morgan felt as if he'd taken a fist to the gut. She was pale and looked like she might be on the verge of tears.

"Are you all right?"

She laughed, but there was no humor to it. "Not really."

He watched a tear slip from the corner of her eye, then slowly trickle down her cheek. The sight of that single droplet just about tore him apart. "Tell me what happened, sweetheart."

"I've learned that in three months the Bureau of Land Management will take possession of my grandfather's ranch," she said, sounding defeated. "And there's absolutely nothing I can do about it."

"But I thought he left everything to you." The knot in Morgan's stomach tightened painfully as he watched her impatiently swipe at a second tear.

"He had another will drawn up a few days before his death," she said, accepting the bandana handkerchief he retrieved from the hip pocket of his jeans.

"Why didn't Greeley know about it?" He hated seeing her so utterly dejected.

She shrugged one shoulder. "My grandfather used the nursing home's attorney because he knew he was dying and Mr. Greeley was out of town. After it had been witnessed and notarized, the administrator of the nursing home accidentally misfiled the will in another resident's folder.'' Her voice broke. ''The mistake...wasn't discovered until the first part of this week...when that man passed away.''

Unable to sit still any longer, Morgan got out of the truck and walked around to the passenger side. Opening the door, he reached inside and wrapped his arms around her.

Samantha immediately buried her face against his shoulder and the flood gates opened. He hated seeing any woman cry, but Samantha's heartbroken sobs were tearing him apart. He wanted to make things better, to fix things for her. But he had no idea where he'd even begin to start on this mess.

When she quieted, he continued to hold her. He enjoyed the feel of her soft body pressed to his too much to let her go.

''Sweetheart, why don't you start at the beginning,'' he finally said. ''Maybe together we can figure out a way for you to keep the property.''

''It's really very simple,'' she said, hiccuping. ''Unless I'm married by September, the Bureau of Land Management will get my grandfather's ranch. And since I don't see that happening—''

''Married?'' Morgan felt like he'd been punched in the gut for the second time in less than ten minutes.

She nodded. ''The will stipulates that I have to be married at the time I claim the property, and that I have to stay married for two years after that before the deed is put in my name.''

"Why in God's name would old Tug do a crazy thing like that to you?" Morgan asked, unable to comprehend the ridiculous terms of the legacy.

"He really wasn't doing it to me," she said, sniffling. "My grandfather wasn't even aware that I existed. Once my mother eloped with my father, she never came back here."

Morgan nodded. "I remember you telling me that he and your mother didn't get along. But in all that time, she never tried to get in touch with Tug?"

"Not that I'm aware of," Samantha said. She sighed heavily as she pulled away from him to open her handbag. Handing him a piece of paper, she added, "Here's the letter explaining his reasoning, although I doubt that I'll ever understand it."

When Morgan scanned the contents of the note, he shook his head in amazement. Tug Shackley's mind must have snapped before he passed on. Either that, or he was the biggest chauvinist the good Lord ever gave the gift of life. At the moment, Morgan wasn't making any bets on which one was the correct answer.

If the heir to Tug's ranch was male, there were no terms to be met, and the property could be claimed immediately. But a female heir had to be married within two years of his death, and stay that way for another two years, before she could claim her inheritance. The letter went on to state that a woman would need a husband to help her restore the ranch to its former productiveness, thus insuring her financial security. But if no heir was found, or a female heir was unmarried by the end of the time limits, the law firm had instructions to donate the land to the BLM in Tug's name.

"Now, I won't even have a connection…to my family through the land, let alone be able to open…the camp," she said, brokenly.

"That's unacceptable." He folded the letter and gave it back to her. "We'll get married this weekend."

As if they were caught in a vacuum, time seemed to come to a complete halt.

He couldn't believe he'd just offered to marry her. But as he stood there gazing into her amber eyes, he realized it was the only thing he could do to help her keep the land that was rightfully hers.

"What did you say?" she finally asked, looking as if he'd taken leave of his senses.

"I said, we'll get married this weekend." He didn't want to dwell on how easily the words rolled off his tongue this time around.

She shook her head. "First it was my grandfather and his stupid stipulations on my inheritance, and now it's you telling me we'll get married." The dubious look in her whiskey-brown eyes left no doubt that she thought his elevator didn't go all the way to the top floor. "Is there something in the water here in Wyoming that makes men go completely insane?"

He placed his hands on her slender shoulders. "Listen to me, Samantha." When he gazed into her amber eyes, he felt as if he might drown. He wanted her. And if they were married…

He swallowed hard and did his best to ignore his wayward thoughts, as well as the sudden tightening south of his belt buckle. "You want to keep your grandfather's ranch to start that children's camp, don't you?"

"Yes, but I can't marry you to do it," she said, her voice shaky.

"Why not?"

"Well, I…that is…" Her voice trailed off and she seemed to be at a loss for words.

"Were there any loopholes?" he asked. "Any way to get around the terms of the will?"

She shook her head. "No. Mr. Greeley said he'd been over it several times, looking for some way for me to keep the land without meeting the terms. But it's quite clear. I have to be married to claim the property."

Morgan gave her shoulders a gentle squeeze. "Then what other choice do you have, Samantha?"

"I…uh, need…to think about this," she said, looking dazed. She massaged her temples with her fingertips. "This is all so bizarre. I have no job, no home and I'm about to lose the only ties I have left to my family, as well as my dream of opening the camp. But if I marry you—"

He could understand her dilemma. If he let himself think about it, he was sure he'd find it pretty unsettling, too. After what happened to Emily, he'd made a vow never to take a trip down the aisle and run the risk of being responsible for another person's well-being.

But this was different. He and Samantha wouldn't be marrying for love, and he wouldn't be responsible for making any decisions for her or little Timmy. They'd lead separate lives, and if they came together from time to time for their physical needs, then where was the harm? They'd be married and it would not only be legal, it would be perfectly moral as well.

"Think about it on the drive home," he said as he stepped back to close the passenger door. Walking around the front of the truck, he got in and started the engine, then reached over to cup her chin in his palm. "We'll work this out, sweetheart. I promise I won't let you lose your land."

Samantha waited until she'd nursed Timmy and put him in the cradle for his afternoon nap before she took a deep breath and headed downstairs to talk to Morgan. Since their discussion in the parking lot, she'd thought of nothing else but the stipulations of her grandfather's will, and the offer Morgan had made to help her meet those terms.

Crossing the great room to the foyer, her legs shook and her insides felt as if they had turned to gelatin. As tempting as it was, she wasn't going to take him up on his offer. She'd learned the hard way not to rely on a man for anything, and she wasn't about to start now. Even if it meant giving up on her dream of starting her camp, she just couldn't do it.

When she reached his office, she took a deep breath and knocked on the frame of the open door. "Are you busy?"

"No." He smiled. "Come in and sit down."

She sank into the armchair across from his desk. "I've reached a decision."

His easy expression faded as he cocked one dark brow. "And that would be?"

"I really appreciate your offer to help me keep the land, but I can't let you put your life on hold for two years," she said, hurrying to get the words out before she changed her mind.

Rising from the chair, he walked around the desk to sit on the edge in front of her. "Samantha, I wouldn't consider it as putting my life on hold. I'd think of it more as helping you, as well as a bunch of kids who got handed a raw deal in life."

Agitated, she stood up to pace. She couldn't let him sway her. "What if you met someone? You'd be tied to me. What happens then?"

"I won't meet anyone," he said, sounding so darned sure that she turned to stare at him.

"You don't know that, Morgan."

"Yes, I do," he said calmly. He crossed his booted feet at the ankles and folded his arms over his wide chest. "You have my word that as long as we're married, I won't so much as look at another woman."

"But the marriage would be in name only," she said, making sure they had that little detail straight.

He shrugged. "That would probably make things simpler."

That hadn't been the answer she'd expected. He was a living, breathing man in his prime. He was going to remain celibate for two years? And how on earth could he be so relaxed about something as important as marriage, even if it wouldn't be a real one?

"Why are you willing to do this for me, Morgan?" she asked, suddenly suspicious of his motives and why he was being so generous. "What's in it for you?"

"Nothing," he said, straightening to his full height. "I just want to see that you and Timmy get what's rightfully yours. And in the bargain, I'll be helping kids who really need it."

"That's it?" She was having a hard time believing that anyone would be that willing to sacrifice their freedom for someone they barely knew.

He nodded, then walked over to take her hands in his. Pulling her to him, he put his arms around her waist. "I want to help you, Samantha. And our getting married is the only way for you to keep your land and start that camp."

She caught her lower lip between her teeth to keep it from trembling. She couldn't believe it, but she was actually thinking about accepting his offer, even though it went against everything she'd vowed never to do again—rely on a man.

As if he sensed she was on the verge of going along with his suggestion, he gave her a smile that curled her toes inside her well-worn tennis shoes. Then, leaning forward, he whispered in her ear, ''What do you say, Samantha? Are you going to marry me, keep your grandfather's ranch and help those kids? Or are you going to turn me down and lose it all?''

How was she supposed to think with him this close? His warm breath was teasing her neck, sending wave after wave of delicious heat skipping over every nerve in her body.

''I'm…not sure…what to do,'' she said, feeling extremely short of breath. His strong hands were splayed across her back, tracing the line of her spine, gently kneading her tense muscles.

''Say yes, Samantha,'' he commanded, kissing the sensitive hollow beneath her ear.

''But—''

He leaned back to stare down at her, his blue gaze intense. ''Yes.''

''Y-yes,'' she finally said, unable to believe she was actually agreeing to become Morgan Wakefield's wife.

Six

Morgan propped his hands on his hips as he looked around the storage area for the old trunk. It had to be here somewhere. His dad had packed all of his mother's things in it shortly after her death, and to Morgan's knowledge it hadn't moved for the past twenty-seven years.

When he spotted the corner of it, he walked over to move several boxes of Christmas ornaments that had been piled on top. Unfastening the clasp, he opened it and gazed down at the contents. The scent of jasmine drifted up from the mementos of his mother's life to flood his senses with memories of the woman who had given him life.

He'd only been seven years old when she passed

away, but he could still remember the feel of her gentle touch when he'd skinned his elbow, the way she'd pressed a soft kiss to his forehead each night when she tucked him into bed, and the smell of her jasmine perfume when she hugged him close. His chest tightened. Even though Hank Wakefield had done a fine job of raising his three sons, and gone out of his way to be both mother and father to them, they'd missed a hell of a lot by not having her with them.

As Morgan dropped down on one knee to begin his search, he felt guilty. It almost felt as if he was invading his mother's privacy. But he somehow knew that she'd approve of what he had in mind and would have probably even suggested it had she been alive.

When he saw the heavy white plastic garment bag close to the bottom of the trunk, he smiled. Removing it, he carefully replaced the rest of his mother's things, then closed the lid and headed back downstairs.

"Samantha?" he called as he descended the steps.

"I'm in the kitchen."

When he walked into the room, she was putting a roast into the oven. Her porcelain cheeks were flushed from the heat and several strands of her golden-brown hair had escaped the confines of her ponytail. He didn't think he'd ever seen her look more attractive.

Handing her the white garment bag, he smiled. "I don't know what size this is, but if it fits, you could wear it on Sunday."

She stared at the bag for several seconds before she gazed up at him. "Was this your mother's?"

He nodded, suddenly unsure about his decision to offer her his mother's wedding dress for the small ceremony they had planned for Sunday afternoon. He knew for a fact that Samantha didn't have the money for a new dress and she'd flat out refused his offer to buy her one. But maybe women didn't like the idea of wearing another woman's dress for their wedding.

"I'll understand if you'd rather wear something else," he said, running his hand over the back of his neck. "I just thought—"

"No, this will be fine," she said, her voice almost a whisper. She lightly ran her fingers over the plastic, as if she touched something precious and fragile. "I would be honored to wear it, Morgan. But don't you think you should save it for after we...that is, when you meet someone else and get married for real?"

"This is most likely the only time I'll ever get married," he said, wishing his statement hadn't sounded quite so blunt.

But he wasn't about to explain his decision to remain a bachelor, or his reasons behind it. It was too complicated, and he didn't think he'd be able to stand the condemnation in Samantha's pretty amber eyes when he told her about his role in Emily's death.

"It will probably be the only time for me, too," she said, surprising him. "I decided after Chad and the choice he made about not wanting anything to do with Timmy, that life alone would be preferable to one filled with heartache. Or worse yet, watching someone disappoint my child the way my father disappointed me.''

It felt as if someone had reached inside his chest and squeezed his heart with a tight fist. How could anyone, no matter who it was, treat Samantha or Timmy as if they didn't matter?

Reaching out, Morgan pulled her into his arms. ''That's one thing you won't have to worry about while you're here at the Lonetree, sweetheart,'' he said. His chest tightened further at the thought of her and the baby eventually leaving to face the world alone. ''I promise I'll never hurt you, or Timmy, and you won't be lonely.''

She stared up at him with guileless amber eyes. ''At least for the next two years?''

''At least,'' he said, nodding as he lowered his mouth to hers.

He didn't want to dwell on the length of their upcoming marriage, or the reason for it. At the moment, the feel of her soft body against his, the scent of her lilac shampoo, and the sound of her soft sigh were sending his libido into overdrive.

Tracing her lips with his tongue, Morgan deepened the kiss to leisurely reacquaint himself with her sweetness, to explore the woman that in two days would become his wife. The thought sent heat streaking through his veins and caused his loins to tighten with need.

When she wrapped her arms around his neck and

leaned into him, Morgan thought his knees were going to buckle. Her firm, full breasts pressed to his chest and the warmth of her lower body cradling the hard ridge of his arousal were almost more than he could stand.

Slowly running his hands up her sides to the swell of her breasts, he cupped the weight of them, then teased the hardened tips through the layers of her clothes. Rewarded by her tiny moan of pleasure, his body responded in a way that made him light-headed. Morgan didn't think he'd ever been as hard in his life as he was at this moment, for this woman.

Knowing that if things went much further, he wouldn't be able to stop, he broke the kiss and took a step back. As he gazed down at her, he decided that wasn't enough distance. She looked so soft, so sweet, that if he didn't move, and damned quick, he'd end up sweeping her into his arms and carrying her upstairs to his bed. And although he was more than ready for it, she wasn't.

"I...really should check on a new colt," he said, turning toward the back door. "If you need help getting that dress ready for Sunday, I'm sure Annie will be more than happy to lend a hand."

Without waiting for her response, he stepped out onto the porch and closed the door behind him. If there had been any doubt in his mind before, it had just been erased.

Taking a deep breath, he tried to get his body to calm down. Their marriage might not be a love match, but the attraction between them was too strong to be denied. There was no way the two of them could live in the same house, day in and day out, without the inevitable happening between them.

It wasn't a matter of if they made love. The question now was, when?

"I knew the first time I saw you and Morgan together that you were made for each other," Annie said, helping Samantha into Morgan's mother's dress.

"You did?" Samantha wondered how on earth her soon-to-be sister-in-law could have gotten that impression.

Annie nodded as she started fastening the tiny buttons that ran from below the waist at the back all the way to the shoulders of the dress. "It's the way you look at each other."

Samantha swallowed hard. She hated that she couldn't tell Annie the real reason behind her and Morgan's decision to get married. But they'd both agreed that the fewer people who knew their marriage was a sham, the better.

As Morgan had pointed out, it wasn't anyone's business but their own. But that still didn't keep Samantha from feeling guilty about not telling Annie.

"Have Colt and Brant made it back from Nashville yet?" she asked, hoping to change the subject. Both brothers had been tied up with a bull-riding event and couldn't make it home until that day.

"They arrived about an hour ago." Annie finished

the last of the buttons and came around to stand in front of her. Tears filled her pretty green eyes. "Oh, Samantha, you look absolutely beautiful."

Staring at herself in the full-length mirror on the back of the closet door, Samantha sighed wistfully. If she'd had her choice of any wedding gown, she knew for certain she would have chosen this one. It was absolutely gorgeous.

With a simple scoop neckline, fitted bodice, cap sleeves, and floor-length skirt flaring from the waist, it was simple, feminine and elegantly traditional. Made of antique white satin overlaid with pure white lace it was everything that Samantha had ever dreamed of wearing for her wedding. That is before she'd stopped dreaming of ever being a bride.

"I think I look scared silly," she said, laughing nervously.

Annie nodded as she arranged a garland of white rosebuds on top of Samantha's head. "I don't think you'd be normal if you weren't nervous." She pinned the headpiece in place, then stood back to admire her handiwork. "Morgan is going to love seeing you come down the stairs in this."

"You think so?" A pang of longing shot through her. Maybe if she and Morgan had met at another time in their lives, and under different circumstances, then things could have been different.

"Absolutely," Annie said, grinning. "He's going to take one look at you and want to carry you back up here before the minister has a chance to perform the ceremony." Before Samantha could find her voice, Annie reached into the shopping bag she'd brought upstairs with her when she first arrived. Pulling a box from the bag, she handed it to Samantha. "Since Morgan was in such a hurry to get you to the altar, I didn't have time to give you a lingerie shower."

Samantha frowned at the Sleek and Sassy Lady Lingerie Boutique logo on the top. "What's this?"

Annie gave her a sly smile. "Oh, just something to make your evening more...um, shall we say, interesting?"

Opening the box to peel back the layers of tissue paper, Samantha's cheeks heated. The skimpiest white lace teddy she'd ever seen lay nestled inside, along with a book on sensual massage and a bottle of scented oil.

"Oh, my!"

"I hope you like it," Annie said, sounding hopeful. "I wore one like this on my wedding night, and..." She blushed prettily. "I was really happy with Brant's reaction. Especially when I used the oil and gave him a massage."

Annie expected her to wear this for Morgan? Tonight? And to rub scented oil all over his body?

Samantha gulped. She felt warm all over at the thought, but she couldn't tell Annie that although they'd shared a few kisses that made her insides feel as if they'd turned to warm pudding, there wouldn't be any nights of grand passion.

A lump formed in her throat and an empty vacant feeling filled her chest. She and Morgan had an agreement, and it was best if they stuck to it.

So why did the thought that they wouldn't be sharing everything a husband and wife shared make her feel so sad? So utterly alone? That's the way she wanted it, wasn't it?

"Thank you, Annie." She replaced the box lid, then set it on top of the dresser. "I think any man with a pulse would like seeing a woman in that."

When Colt punched the button on the CD player, and George Strait started singing about crossing his heart and promising that his love was truer than any other, Morgan's stomach churned like a cement mixer gone berserk. What the hell did he think he was doing?

Six years ago, he'd vowed never to get married—never to be responsible for another person's wellbeing. Yet, here he stood, waiting for Samantha to come down the stairs and join him in front of the fireplace in the great room so Preacher Hill from the Methodist church down in Bear Creek could pronounce them man and wife.

Reminding himself this was the only way to help her keep the land that was rightfully hers, Morgan reached up to put his index finger in the collar of his dress shirt. He gave it a tug in an effort to create a little more space between the restrictive top button and his Adam's apple. Why did a suit and tie always make a man feel like he had a noose around his damned neck?

"Relax, bro. Being married is the best thing that ever happened to me," Brant said as Annie appeared at the top of the staircase, holding Timmy. Grinning he asked, "Have you ever seen a woman prettier than my Annie?"

Morgan opened his mouth to tell his brother he sounded like a lovesick teenager, but the words lodged in his throat. Samantha stood at the top of the steps, her silky, golden-brown hair swept up in a cascade of loose curls, her whiskey-colored eyes gazing at him like he was the only man in the room. Wearing his mother's wedding dress, and carrying a single white rose, he'd never seen her look more beautiful.

He swallowed hard as he stared up at the woman he was about to marry. "Annie's almost as pretty as Samantha."

"I think I'm gonna puke," Colt muttered under his breath. "You two are about the saddest cases I've ever seen."

"Can it, little brother," Morgan said, unable to take his eyes off of Samantha as she and Annie descended the stairs. "You're lucky we didn't make you skip down the stairs scattering flower petals."

Colt snorted. "Yeah, like that would ever happen." He shook his head. "I'm never going to get as moon-eyed over a woman as you two."

"Your day is coming," Brant warned, stepping forward to escort his wife and Timmy over to the fireplace.

Morgan's heart pounded hard against his rib cage and his knees felt as if they might fail him at any second when he moved toward the stairs to wait for Samantha. But the moment she reached the bottom step and trustingly placed her hand in his, a calm swept over him that he couldn't explain, nor did he want to.

"You look beautiful," he said, gazing down into her pretty eyes.

She smiled and Morgan could have sworn it chased the late afternoon shadows from the room. "I was just thinking how handsome you look," she said, touching the lapel of his black western-cut suit jacket.

"Are you ready for this?" he asked, tucking her hand in the crook of his arm.

She took a deep breath and nodded. "I guess so."

Leading her over to where Preacher Hill stood in front of the big stone fireplace, Morgan glanced at the baby sleeping peacefully in Annie's arms, then at Samantha. He was about to take on a wife and child. But instead of striking fear in his heart and sending him running like hell in the opposite direction as it would have six weeks ago, the thought filled him with a deep satisfaction that defied explanation or logic.

"Dearly beloved, we are gathered here today to join this man and this woman…" Preacher Hill began.

As the ceremony progressed, Morgan felt a twinge

of guilt when it came time to repeat the traditional words that would make them husband and wife. He hated to lie about anything, but especially when it came to something as sacred as wedding vows. There was no doubt that he would honor and cherish Samantha. But he'd just promised to love her and stay with her until death.

He swallowed hard. Why hadn't they thought about writing their own vows? They could have skirted around those issues.

But when he heard her promise to love, honor and cherish him in return, a satisfied warmth flowed through him. The thought of having her with him, loving him for the rest of his life lit the darkest corners of his soul. And at the moment, he wasn't about to remind himself that their arrangement was only temporary.

When the stoic, elderly preacher requested the rings, Morgan gave him the wedding bands that he'd made a special trip to Laramie to purchase the day before. Handing the smaller one back, the good reverend instructed him to put the ring on the third finger of Samantha's left hand and repeat the words that would make her his.

"With this ring—" he caught and held her gaze as he slid the shiny, wide gold band onto her trembling finger "—I thee wed."

"When did you get these?" she whispered, her eyes shiny with unshed tears.

"Yesterday," he said, bringing her hand to his mouth to press a kiss to the ring circling her finger.

Preacher Hill handed her the other wedding band, and as she slid it onto his finger and repeated the traditional words, a lone tear slowly trickled down her cheek. "By the power vested in me by God, and the state of Wyoming, I now pronounce you husband and wife," the man said. "Son, kiss your bride."

Samantha held her breath as Morgan reached up to wipe the tear sliding down her cheek with the pad of his thumb, then drew her into his arms to seal their union with a kiss that made her insides quiver and caused her mind to reel from everything that had taken place in the last few minutes.

She'd just promised to love Morgan, to stay with him no matter what. How on earth would she be able to walk away from him in two years after pledging something like that?

"You might want to let her up for air," Brant said, laughing as he slapped Morgan on the shoulder. "Welcome to the world of the blissfully hitched, bro."

When Morgan lifted his head to smile at her, tiny electrical impulses skipped over every nerve in her body. If she didn't know better, she'd think he intended for them to...

"If this big galoot doesn't tow the line, just let me know," Brant said. He pushed Morgan aside to hug her and place a brotherly kiss on her cheek. "I'll be more than happy to kick his butt for you."

"I'll remember that," she said, smiling wanly.

The Wakefields were so nice she really hated deceiving them. But they had no way of knowing the marriage was only temporary, and not an everlasting commitment of love and devotion.

"My turn to kiss the bride," Colt said, shouldering Brant out of the way and making a show of really getting into the act. But when Morgan cleared his throat and sent a dark scowl his way, Colt grinned and lightly pressed his lips to her other cheek. "It's good to meet you, Samantha. Welcome to the family."

When her new brother-in-law mentioned the one thing that she'd always wanted—to be part of a family—she couldn't shake the deep sadness that washed over her. Although her last name had just become Wakefield, it was all pretend. She wasn't, and never would be, a real part of their family.

Morgan must have sensed her discomfort, because he put his arms around her waist to pull her close. "You and Timmy *are* part of us now, sweetheart," he whispered close to her ear.

"Thank you," was all she could manage as she fought to hold back her tears.

Once the minister filled out the marriage certificate, had Brant and Annie sign in the appropriate place as witnesses to the marriage and excused himself to drive back to Bear Creek, Annie took charge. Placing Timmy in his baby carrier, she instructed, "Brant, you and Colt watch the baby while I get everything ready in the kitchen.'' Turning to Morgan and Samantha, she added, ''You two take a little time to catch your breath and get ready for pictures and cutting the cake.''

''Pictures?'' Morgan looked as surprised as Samantha felt.

''Cake?'' She hadn't counted on Annie going to so much trouble.

Nodding, Annie grinned. ''You'll want pictures to reminisce over when you celebrate your fiftieth anniversary. And it's not official until you smear cake all over each other's face.''

Before Samantha found her voice to ask if Annie needed help in the kitchen, her new sister-in-law breezed down the hall and out of sight.

As Colt and Brant stared down at Timmy like they weren't quite sure what they were supposed to do, Morgan asked, ''Are you doing okay?''

''I'm not sure,'' she said honestly. ''It's hard to take in all that's happened in the last hour.''

He smiled. ''Feels like you've been hit by a train, doesn't it?''

She nodded, as she watched her two brothers-in-law gaze down at her son. ''I just hate that we're deceiving them.''

''Are we?''

Samantha sucked in a sharp breath and turned to stare at him. ''What do you mean?''

''Everything's ready for the pictures and cutting the cake,'' Annie said, walking back into the room before

Morgan could answer. "Brant, you get our camera. Colt, you're in charge of the baby."

"Me?" Colt sounded alarmed. "I don't know what to do with a baby."

"Take hold of the carrier's handle and bring him into the kitchen," Annie said, patiently. "Believe me, he won't bite."

"He might," Colt said, eyeing Timmy carefully. "He doesn't look like he likes me very much."

"You end up growing on people. Sort of like a fungus," Brant said, laughing as he picked up the camera from the slate coffee table.

Colt looked insulted. "Thanks a lot. What kind of impression do you think that gives our new sister-in-law?"

"She'll get used to you, just like the rest of us had to," Brant said. "And don't worry about the baby biting. If he does decide to give you a little nip, it won't hurt. He doesn't have teeth yet."

"So now that Annie's pregnant you're an expert on babies, huh?" Colt groused as he picked up the baby carrier and followed his brother down the hall.

Morgan took Samantha's hand. "Come on. Let's get this over with so they'll leave and I can get out of this damned monkey suit."

Samantha didn't budge. "I think we need to discuss the issue of your questioning our deception."

"We'll talk later," he said, giving her a kiss that left her absolutely breathless. "Now smile, sweetheart. This is your wedding day."

Seven

For the next half hour, Samantha felt as if she was living a dream. Morgan played the role of the attentive groom, while Brant, instructed by Annie, snapped so many pictures Samantha wasn't sure she'd ever be able to see again without spots dancing before her eyes.

"Time to cut the cake," Annie finally announced.

"Were you, by any chance, a wedding planner before you married Brant?" Samantha asked as Annie showed her and Morgan where and how to cut the cake.

"No, I was a librarian." Annie grinned as she added, "But one of my favorite books was *How to Plan a Fairytale Wedding*."

Samantha laughed. "It shows."

Taking the decorative knife, her breath caught and heat coursed through her veins as Morgan covered her hand with his and they sliced the beautiful white wedding cake Annie had bought at a bakery in Laramie. Samantha tried to ignore the feeling.

But when they fed each other a small piece, and Morgan licked the icing from her fingers, there was no way she could dismiss the delicious fluttery feeling deep in the pit of her stomach. Nor could she deny the fact that every cell in her being tingled to life.

She had to get a grip on herself. It was as if she'd forgotten that this was just an act—a show for the benefit of his family.

After everyone had a piece of wedding cake, Annie enlisted Brant and Colt's help, and in no time they had everything put away and the kitchen spotless.

"Colt is spending the night with us," Annie announced as she tugged on his sleeve.

Colt frowned. "I am?"

"Yes, you are," Brant said, elbowing his younger brother in the ribs and treating him to a meaningful look.

"Oh, right." Colt's grin caused Samantha's cheeks to feel as if they were on fire. "Just in case you're tired and want to sleep in tomorrow morning, I won't be back until noon to get my stuff. After that I'll be taking off for Mitch's place."

Annie stepped forward to hug Samantha. "I'd offer to watch the baby for you, but since you're nursing,

I know you can't be away from each other for that long."

Nodding, Samantha hugged her new sister-in-law back. "Thank you for everything, Annie. I truly appreciate your thoughtfulness."

"We're sisters now, and I was happy to do it." Lowering her voice, she added, "Don't forget to wear the teddy. I promise Morgan's reaction will be well worth it." Turning to her husband and brother-in-law, she motioned toward the door. "Come on you two. It's time we left the newlyweds alone."

No sooner had the three of them walked out the back door, than Timmy let out a wail, indicating that he wanted to nurse again.

Samantha was thankful for the excuse to have a little time to herself, in order to come to terms with all that had taken place. It wasn't every day a woman got married to one of the sexiest men alive, only to plan on spending her wedding night completely alone.

Lifting her son from the baby carrier, she started toward the stairs. "I'll come back down later and get the baby carrier."

"I'll get it," Morgan said, impatiently tugging on the knot of his tie. "While you're taking care of Timmy, I'm going to change into something that doesn't make me feel like I'm being throttled."

"I should change, too," she said, hoping Timmy didn't spit up before she could take off her borrowed dress. "This gown is beautiful, but—" She groaned as she suddenly thought of how much trouble it would be to get out of it. "Oh, no. I forgot to have Annie help me with the back."

Morgan shoved the necktie in one of the pockets of his suit coat and worked the top two buttons loose on his shirt. "I'll help you once we get upstairs."

Before she could think of some other way to get the dress unbuttoned, he took the baby carrier in one hand and guided her to the stairs with the other. Helping her climb the stairs without tripping on the long skirt, he opened the door to the room she shared with Timmy, then set the baby carrier on the window seat while she laid Timmy on the bed.

When he stepped up behind her, Samantha caught her breath and her stomach felt as if it did a somersault at the first touch of his hands at her shoulders. Having him unfasten the back of her dress seemed so intimate, so husbandlike.

"Damn, these things are little, and there's about a hundred of them," he said, his deep voice sending a wave of longing straight through her.

As he worked the buttons through the tiny loops, his fingers brushed her spine, and with each touch, heat streaked straight to the pit of her stomach. To distract herself, Samantha shook her head and tried to concentrate on what he'd said.

"I think there are only thirty or forty buttons," she said, trying not to sound as breathless as she felt. "But you're right, they are tiny."

When he reached the last few, the ones at the small of her back, his fingers lingered a bit longer with each one. Shivers of excitement shot through her and she found it extremely difficult to draw a breath.

What on earth had she gotten herself into? Had she lost her mind when she agreed to marry him?

Each time Morgan touched her, her body zinged to life and she was in serious danger of melting into a puddle at his big booted feet. How was she ever going to survive two years of living under the same roof with him and not give in to the sizzling tension between them?

"There you go," he said, his warm breath tickling the back of her neck and causing the heat inside of her to intensify.

Holding the dress to keep it from falling off her shoulders, she quickly stepped away from him. "Th-thank you."

His sexy smile and hooded sapphire gaze sent another wave of awareness skimming over every nerve in her body. "Samantha, we need to talk about—"

Impatient for his next meal, Timmy let them know that he was tired of waiting by wailing at the top of his lungs.

"He needs to nurse," she said, thankful for the interruption.

She had a good idea what Morgan wanted to discuss, and she needed time to collect herself. They were going to have to establish some ground rules to keep from doing something that would greatly complicate their situation.

To her surprise, instead of being upset that Timmy

needed her, Morgan leaned down to tickle the baby's stomach. "I'll see you later, little guy." Walking to the door, he turned back to face her. "It's late. Do you think he'll sleep for a while?"

"I—" she swallowed hard "—think so."

Morgan nodded. "Good. We'll have plenty of time to…talk."

Once he'd changed into more comfortable clothes, Morgan carried his boots in one hand as he padded down the hall in his socks to Samantha's door. He'd been so turned on by the simple act of unbuttoning her dress, of feeling her soft skin beneath his fingers, he'd forgotten to tell her to meet him in his office after she got the baby down for the night.

He shook his head. It was important that they get a few things worked out about their arrangement. He needed to make it clear that although they were married, he wouldn't be responsible for any decisions she made concerning her or Timmy's welfare.

Tapping on the oak door frame, he waited a second then opened the door and walked into the room. "Samantha, I'll be down in my office when—"

He stopped short and his boots hit the floor with a loud clunk at the sight of her sitting in the rocking chair holding Timmy. She'd changed out of his mother's wedding gown and put on a pale yellow dress made of soft-looking gauzy fabric. But what held him riveted to the spot was the fact that the dress was open to the waist and the baby was nursing her breast. Morgan had never seen a more poignant sight in his entire thirty-four years.

"Morgan, what do you think you're doing?" Samantha asked, her startled movement pulling her nipple from Timmy's mouth.

The dark coral tip was wet and shiny, and Morgan couldn't have looked away if his life depended on it. "I…" He had to stop to clear the rust from his throat. "…wanted to tell you that I'll be waiting for you in my office."

His evening meal interrupted, Timmy protested loudly.

Morgan swallowed hard as he watched her guide her breast back to the baby's lips, then drape a small blanket over herself and the baby's face. Fascinated, he asked, "Does that hurt?"

She stared at him for several long moments, then slowly shook her head. "It did at first, but that was before I got used to breastfeeding."

He walked over to kneel down beside the rocking chair, then holding her gaze with his, he slowly reached up to move the soft blanket aside. When she didn't try to stop him, he glanced down to see Timmy's mouth working rhythmically to drink his mother's milk.

"I've watched thousands of animals nurse, but this is the first time I've seen a woman nurse a child." He'd never been one for putting his feelings into words, and he figured he should probably shut up now before he made a fool of himself, but the moment was so special, he had to let her know. "It's beautiful."

For the next several minutes they both remained silent as Samantha nursed the baby and Morgan watched.

"He's asleep," she finally said, her voice little more than a whisper.

Without asking, Morgan lifted Timmy into his arms and cradled him to his chest while Samantha covered herself. "Do you want me to put him in the cradle?"

She nodded. "He should sleep until four or five tomorrow morning."

Rising to his feet, Morgan placed the sleeping baby in the cradle that had rocked three generations of Wakefield boys, then waited for Samantha to cover her son with a downy soft blanket. When she turned to face him, he thought he'd drown in the depths of her whiskey-brown eyes.

"Things have changed," he said, taking her left hand in his.

She stared at him for several long seconds before she lowered her gaze to their hands. "This isn't smart."

"Probably not." He ran the pad of his thumb over the shiny gold band circling her finger, reminding himself and her, that she was his.

"We agreed the marriage wouldn't be real," she said, lifting her head to look at him.

"Not really." He took her hands and placed them on his shoulders, then wrapped his arms around her waist to draw her forward. "*You* said the marriage would be in name only."

"And you agreed." She sounded breathless.

"No, I didn't." He leaned his forehead against hers. "I said it would probably be for the best. But technically, I never agreed to those terms."

Before she could respond, Morgan lowered his mouth to hers and once again tasted her sweetness, reveled in the feel of her soft curves against him. The spark that seemed to have been smoldering in his gut since the day they first met, ignited into a flame and tightened his lower body with a swiftness that left him dizzy. He'd never wanted a woman more in his life than he wanted Samantha.

Gently pushing his tongue past her lips, he stroked and explored her inner recesses. He loved the taste of her, the shy eagerness of her response when he ran his hands down to cup her bottom and draw her into the cradle of his hips. Her moan of pleasure at the feel of his arousal pressed to her soft lower belly sent his blood pressure up a good twenty points and had his heart hammering wildly against his ribs.

Lifting his head, he asked, "Can you honestly say we'll be able to live together for two years without making love, sweetheart?"

He watched her close her eyes for a moment, then opening them to stare up at him, she lifted her arms to encircle his neck and tangle her fingers in the hair at the nape of his neck. "We should try."

"Two years is a long time." He pulled her closer,

letting her feel how much he wanted her. "Do you really want to keep this marriage in name only?"

She trembled against him. "I...I've probably lost my mind, but I'm not sure anymore."

"What do you really want, Samantha?" he asked, bringing his hands up to cup her full breasts.

When he teased the tips through the layers of her clothes, she sighed softly. "Kiss me again, Morgan. I want you to kiss me again."

"It'll be my pleasure," he said as he reached up to free her hair from the clip holding it off of her neck. "And I'm going to make damned sure it's yours, too."

Samantha's eyes fluttered shut as Morgan's mouth covered hers in a kiss that robbed her of breath, and what little sense she had left. She didn't want to think about how insane it would be to make their marriage real, or the fact that in two years, it would be over. The need to feel wanted, to be cherished by him as only a man can cherish a woman, was far stronger than the thought of the complications they would face later.

As Morgan ran his hands over her back, shivers of anticipation coursed through her. But when he plunged his tongue past her lips to claim her with sure, confident strokes, her knees began to wobble and she shamelessly clung to his solid strength for support.

Lifting his head to stare down at her with his incredible blue eyes, he smiled. "What do you want now, sweetheart?"

She took a deep breath as she tried to slow her rapidly beating pulse. "I don't think I want you to stop."

His deep chuckle sent a wave of goose bumps shimmering over her skin. "I don't think either one of us want that." He nuzzled the side of her neck, sending shivers of delight coursing to her very core. "Did the doctor put you on any kind of birth control when you went for your checkup?" he asked, his voice low and intimate.

"I…um, no. I hadn't planned on being married…let alone making love." How was she supposed to think with him so close, with his firm lips nibbling tiny kisses at the hollow behind her ear?

He raised his head to gaze down at her, and the look in his eyes sent her temperature skyward. "Don't worry, sweetheart. I'll take care of it." Giving her a quick kiss, he took her hand in his, switched on the baby monitor, then picked up the listening unit. "Why don't we go to my room?"

As she let Morgan lead her down the hall to his bedroom, her heart hammered inside her chest and she had to remind herself to breathe.

Once they made love, there was no turning back. Their marriage would be real and everything would be much more complex. Was that really what she wanted?

And what happened at the end of the two year requirement for her to gain control of her land? Was there a chance she and Morgan would stay together?

"It's going to be all right, Samantha," Morgan said as they entered his room. He switched on the bedside lamp, set the baby monitor on the table, then turned to cup her face with his large palms. "I'm not making any demands on you. If you want to call a halt to this right now, we will."

She searched his handsome features. God help her, she'd probably live to regret it, but she didn't have the strength to take him up on the retreat he'd offered her. Didn't even want to. She wanted his touch, the taste of his kiss and the warmth of his lovemaking.

"No," she said, surprised at how steady and sure her voice sounded. "I don't want to stop."

The heated look in his amazing blue eyes warmed her all the way to her toes as he lowered his head and kissed her with a gentleness that brought tears to her eyes. "I promise you won't regret it, sweetheart."

When he reached up to unbutton her dress, his gaze held her captive and she had to force herself to breathe. "I think I'd better warn you…I haven't lost all of the weight I gained while I was pregnant."

She watched his eyes darken as he shook his head. "I like the way you look. A woman is supposed to have rounded curves."

Figuring he might as well be aware of all of her flaws, she added, "I also have a few stretch marks."

"I've got a few scars of my own, sweetheart." He worked the last button open, then trailed his finger up to her breasts. "You have no idea how extremely sexy you are, do you?"

"I've never—" when he released the front clasp of her bra, she had to stop and force air into her lungs "—thought of myself as sexy."

"You should," he said, pushing her dress and the straps of her bra from her shoulders. "You're the most desirable woman I've ever known."

As he cupped her breasts in his calloused palms, Samantha's heart rate doubled and she felt as if her insides had turned to melted butter. Closing her eyes, she concentrated on the feel of his rough hands on her body, the tingles of excitement that surged through her when he teased her nipples with the pads of his thumbs.

"Does that feel good?" he asked, kissing her forehead, her eyes and the tip of her nose.

"Y-yes."

She opened her eyes and bringing her hands up to the front of his chambray shirt began to unfasten the snaps. When she parted the shirt to reveal his well-muscled chest, her breath caught. Morgan Wakefield was perfect.

His chest muscles were well developed and the wall of his abdomen rippled from years of physical labor. A fine coating of black hair covered his chest, then thinned out to a fine line arrowing down to his navel and beyond. Samantha's gaze followed the stripe to where it disappeared below the waistband of his well-worn jeans.

"You're gorgeous," she whispered, placing her hands on the hard sinew. She ran her fingers over the thick pads of his pectoral muscles, lingering on the small flat disks that puckered and beaded from her touch.

Glancing up, the heat she saw in his blue gaze sent an answering warmth to the pit of her stomach and had her bare toes curling into the thick carpet. Without a word he lowered his head to kiss the slope of her breasts, then grazed each nipple with his tongue. Threads of desire began to wind their way through her and caused her breath to come out in short little puffs.

"You're the one who's beautiful," he murmured against her sensitized skin. He kissed the tips, then looked up at her. "I want to see all of you, Saman-tha."

His low, suggestive voice caused a delightful little flutter in her lower belly and made her knees feel as if they were about to fold. "I want to see you, too."

Smiling encouragingly, he slowly pushed her dress downward and in no time at all the loose garment lay in a pool of gauzy cotton at her feet. He placed his hands on her hips to steady her as she stepped away from it.

"My turn?" she asked, bringing her hands to the waistband of his jeans.

When he nodded, she worked the button through the buttonhole, then slowly, carefully pulled the metal tab down over the hard ridge of his arousal. Fascinated by the strength and power straining insistently against his white cotton briefs, she traced her finger along the warm bulge.

"Sweetheart, I'll give you all night to quit that," Morgan said with a groan.

"That sounds interesting," she said, wondering if that throaty female voice was really hers.

"Oh, I can guarantee you're not going to be bored." His low voice and meaningful look held such promise that goose bumps shimmied up her arms.

Before she could touch him again, he stepped back. Shrugging out of his shirt, he shoved his jeans and briefs down his muscular thighs, then removed his thick white socks. Straightening to his full height, he stood before her like a perfectly sculpted statue come to life.

Samantha didn't think she'd ever seen anything quite as magnificent as Morgan Wakefield. With impossibly wide shoulders, muscular arms and lean flanks, he looked like a Greek god. As her gaze drifted lower, her eyes widened and her breath caught. Make that an impressively aroused Greek god.

He closed the gap separating them, then giving her a smile that sent her temperature up a good ten degrees, he hooked his thumbs in the waistband of her sensible cotton panties, and quickly removed the last barrier between them. She suddenly felt shy and extremely vulnerable.

"Could we...turn off the lamp?" she asked hesitantly.

"Why, sweetheart?"

"I'm not exactly—"

He gently touched her cheek with one long, masculine finger. "I've seen you before, sweetheart. You're beautiful."

Samantha felt as if her cheeks were on fire. "You were supposed to forget the night Timmy was born. I wasn't exactly at my best."

Morgan shook his head. "I can't forget. It was one of the most meaningful nights of my life."

His answer shocked her. "It was?"

Smiling, he nodded. "I've always thought women were pretty special. But helping you give birth to Timmy left me with a deeper appreciation of a woman's strength and courage. I'm in awe of you, Samantha."

Before she could find her voice, he pulled her into his arms and the feel of him against her, the contrast of masculine hair-roughened flesh to smooth feminine skin caused her to forget anything she'd been about to say. A current seemed to flow between them, charging her with a need deeper than anything she'd ever experienced.

"You feel so damned good, I think I could stand here like this forever," he said, sounding out of breath.

She brought her arms up to circle his shoulders. "I hope you're strong enough to hold both of us upright because I think I'm about to collapse."

His deep chuckle sent a shiver of anticipation right

to her core. "As good as it feels to hold you against me like this, it's going to feel even better for both of us when I'm inside you."

His candid comment sent a wave of longing pulsing through every cell in her being. Releasing her, he pulled the comforter and sheet back, then lifted her as if she weighed nothing at all, and laid her on his bed.

When he stretched out beside her, he gently ran his index finger down between her breasts, then continued on to her navel. "Are these the places you were talking about?" he asked, tracing the marks left by her pregnancy.

She nodded. "I hope they don't take too long to fade."

He propped himself up on one elbow, then leaned down to press his lips to each one of the uneven lines. "Wear them with pride, sweetheart. They're badges of courage."

The reverence in his deep voice, his firm lips tenderly touching her, caused her heart to fill with an emotion she wasn't quite ready to acknowledge. If she didn't know better, she'd swear she was falling for him.

Before she could fully comprehend the threat that might represent to her peace of mind, Morgan moved to gather her into his arms. His lips covering hers chased away all thought and quickly had her feeling as if the world had been reduced to nothing but this man and this moment.

He slid his calloused palm over her ribs, then down to her hip. A shiver of delight streaked up her spine. But when he moved his hand along the inside of her leg to find the moist heat at the juncture of her thighs, a pulsing need began to pool deep in the pit of her stomach. Parting her, he gently tested her readiness as he deepened the kiss.

Wanting to touch him as he touched her, Samantha ran her hand over his flat belly to his lean flank and beyond. When she found him and stroked him with the same infinite care, a groan of pleasure rumbled up from deep in his chest.

"Easy, sweetheart," he said, his voice strained. "It's been a while and I don't want this over with before we get started."

"Please—"

"Do you want me inside?" he asked, his gaze capturing hers as he continued to tease her.

"Y-yes," she said breathlessly. "Please make love to me, Morgan."

Giving her a smile that caused the empty ache of need within her to intensify, he arranged their protection, then moved over her. "I'm going to try to take this slow, Samantha," he said, propping himself up on his elbows. "But I want you so damned much, I'm not sure I'll be able to." He leaned down to give her a kiss so tender it brought tears to her eyes as he parted her legs with one muscular thigh. "The book said that some women find lovemaking uncomfortable the first time after giving birth." He brushed a strand of her hair from her cheeks with his index finger. "If there's even a hint of discomfort, I want you to tell me. You got that?"

His concern touched her in ways she'd never imagined, and if she could have found her voice she would have told him so. But all she could manage was a quick nod before he pressed forward and she felt the exquisite stretching of his body merging with hers. She bit her lower lip to keep from moaning her pleasure as she savored the feeling of being filled by Morgan.

"You feel so damned good," he said as he sank all of himself into her.

She watched his jaw tighten as he closed his eyes and she instinctively knew he was having to dig deep for the strength to maintain his control.

When he finally opened his eyes, he gathered her into his arms. "Are you all right, sweetheart? Am I hurting you?"

"It…feels wonderful," she said breathlessly.

"Are you sure?"

"I couldn't be more certain," she said, placing her hand along his lean jaw at the same time she tilted her hips into his. She watched his brilliant gaze darken at the movement. "Make love to me, Morgan."

He gave her a smile that made her feel like she was the most desired woman alive as he lowered his mouth to hers. Pulling back, then slowly pushing his hips forward, he set an easy pace and in no time Samantha felt the coil of need inside of her tighten, felt herself tense in anticipation of the mind-shattering release.

Morgan must have sensed she was close because he reached down to touch her tiny pleasure point, encouraging her to take everything that he offered. Without warning she was suddenly tumbling, free-falling through a mist of warm, wonderful sensations.

A moment later, she felt Morgan's big body stiffen, then shudder as he gave into his own climax. Wrapping her arms around his wide shoulders, she bit her lower lip and held him to her as she tried to fight the emotion building deep inside of her.

For her well-being, and for Timmy's, she couldn't allow herself to fall in love with Morgan Wakefield, couldn't let herself count on him returning her feelings. If she did, and he turned out to be like her father, or Chad, she wasn't sure she'd be able to survive the devastation of having him reject her.

Eight

When Morgan finally found the strength to move, he started to lever himself away from her, but she hugged him tighter. "I'm too heavy for you, Samantha."

"I like the way you feel," she whispered against his shoulder.

Chuckling, he held her as he rolled to one side, taking her with him. "I like the way you feel, too." He kissed her cute little nose. "Are you okay?"

The tears filling her eyes scared him as little else could. "I'm...wonderful."

"Then why are you crying?" he asked, wiping a tear from her cheek. He wasn't sure, but he hoped like hell it was one of those times when a woman cried because something was meaningful to her.

"Making love with you was beautiful," she said, sending a wave of relief coursing through him.

He smiled. "You had me scared there for a minute, sweetheart."

The sound of an awakening baby suddenly filtered into the room from the monitor on the bedside table.

"Timmy may need to nurse some more," she said, starting to draw away from him.

Morgan shook his head as he rose from the bed and pulled on his briefs. "You stay here and rest. I'll go get the baby."

Quickly padding down the hall in his bare feet, Morgan entered the room where Timmy was raising nine kinds of hell. He grinned as he lifted the crying baby to his shoulder. Morgan liked the way Timmy smelled, the way his tiny body fit into the palms of his hands.

"Thanks for timing that just right, little guy," he said, gently rubbing Timmy's back.

When Morgan re-entered his bedroom, Samantha was sitting up in bed with the sheet tucked under her arms, her luscious breasts hidden from his appreciative gaze. "He's probably hungry," she said, holding her arms out.

"Wait just a second," he said, handing the baby to her.

She gave him a curious look. "Why?"

"You'll see." He gathered the pillows, propped them against the headboard, then sat down beside her. Pulling her onto his lap, he cradled her to his chest much as she cradled Timmy. "Are you comfortable, sweetheart?"

"Y-yes," she said, looking even more confused.

"Good." He smiled as he peeled the sheet back to reveal her full breasts. "I'm going to hold you while you nurse Timmy."

Tears filled her expressive amber eyes. "You're a very special man, Morgan Wakefield."

"Nah, I just like holding you," he said, settling back against the pillows. He watched as she guided her nipple to the baby's mouth. "Samantha?"

"Hmm?"

"I want you to move yours and Timmy's things in here tomorrow morning," he said, surprising even himself. But the more he thought about it, the more it made sense. He wanted her with him—warming his bed, warming him.

She gazed up at him for endless seconds. "But our marriage isn't—"

"It is now," he said, smiling down at her.

He could tell there were several questions running through her mind. Truth to tell, he was probably asking himself the same things. But at the moment, he didn't have answers for either one of them. All he knew was that it felt right.

When Samantha yawned, he kissed the top of her head. "I'll move the cradle in here tomorrow morning."

She closed her eyes and snuggled against him. "We'll see," she said sleepily.

With his arms wrapped around her, Morgan gazed down at the woman and baby cradled in his arms. Both had fallen sound asleep. A possessive feeling like nothing he'd ever known filled his chest and made him want to protect and take care of them.

He sucked in a sharp breath and his heart began to hammer hard against his ribs. What had gotten into him? He couldn't be responsible for either one of them. He'd proven six years ago that his judgment was faulty. What if he made a wrong decision and jeopardized their welfare?

Closing his eyes, he leaned his head back against the headboard. What had he been thinking when he'd pushed Samantha to make their marriage real? Had he lost his mind and allowed his lust to override common sense?

He forced himself to breathe in, then breathe out. He'd blamed his wanting Samantha on the long, cold winter he'd spent alone in this same bed and the need for physical release. But in the past six weeks, he'd had more than one opportunity to make a trip down to Buffalo Gals, and he'd passed every time.

Swallowing around the fear clogging his throat, he opened his eyes to look down at them. Could he live with this woman and her child for the next two years without getting more involved than he already was?

When he first brought her home from the hospital, he'd tried to keep his distance. But that hadn't worked. He'd only ended up working himself into exhaustion during the day and spent every night lying awake, thinking about her sleeping right down the hall.

Would sharing his days with her, then making love to her every night get her out of his system? Or would it only whet his appetite for the life he'd always wanted, but couldn't trust himself to have? Would it only end up complicating everything in ways that he'd never be able to straighten out?

After Emily died, he'd vowed never to take on the responsibility of having a wife and family, of making the decisions that could mean the difference between life and death for them. He glanced down at his wife and her son. He'd promised to help Samantha get her land, and he'd be damned before he went back on his word. But could he live with them, play the role of husband and father, and still keep from investing himself emotionally?

Unable to come up with any answers, Morgan shook his head. He wasn't sure. The only thing he did know for certain was that he'd have to try. For their sake, and his.

Samantha nibbled on her lower lip as she emptied the dresser drawers in the room she and Timmy had shared for the past six weeks. Had she made the right decision about moving into Morgan's room?

Last night she'd become his wife in every sense of the word, but that would be ending once she met the terms of her grandfather's will. A lump the size of her fist clogged her throat at the thought.

"After we move the rest of your clothes, I'll put your suitcases in the storage room," Morgan said, returning to carry more of her things to his bedroom. He came up behind her to rest his hands on her shoulders. "After Colt finally shows up, we'll move the cradle, then go down to the machine shed and get the rest of your stuff from your car."

A delightful shiver slipped up her spine when he pressed his lips to the nape of her neck. "That's fine," she said, turning to face him. Searching his handsome face, she asked, "Are we doing the right thing?"

She held her breath when he remained silent for several long moments. "Samantha, I can't honestly answer that," he admitted. "I've made no secret of the fact that I want you." He smiled as he wrapped his arms around her waist. "And I can tell you want me. But I want you to know that even though you're my wife, you still have the freedom to make your own choices. I can't decide what's best for you and Timmy. I won't even try."

"I'm not sure I'm capable of that either," she said, bowing her head. She suddenly felt very tired and unsure of everything.

He placed his index finger beneath her chin and lifted her head until their gazes met. "All I can promise you for sure is that I'll provide for you and Timmy, and I'll never intentionally hurt either one of you in any way."

She forced a smile. "At least for the next two years."

His expression suddenly unreadable, he slowly nodded. "At least."

They continued to stare at each other for what seemed an eternity, until the sound of booted feet climbing the stairs, followed by a succinct curse caught their attention. "Hey, Morgan, where the hell are you?" a male voice called.

"Down here in the guest room," Morgan answered. He kissed the tip of her nose. "Do you still want us to move the cradle?"

Thinking of how gently he'd made love to her, how tenderly he'd held her while she nursed Timmy the night before, she found herself nodding. "Yes."

"What are you doing in here?" Colt asked as he walked into the room. He came to a halt, then looking sheepish, shook his head. "Don't answer that. I think I know."

"You don't know squat, little brother," Morgan said, giving her a quick kiss before he released her. "We're moving Samantha and the baby into my room."

"How's my nephew today?" Colt asked, walking over to the cradle. "Still no teeth?"

At the reference to her son being his nephew, Samantha's chest tightened. As long as she was married to Morgan, Timmy had the one thing she'd always wanted for her child—he had a family he belonged to.

"No, he still doesn't have teeth," she said, touched that her new brother-in-law already considered Timmy a part of the Wakefield clan.

"Come on, hotshot," Morgan said, clamping his hand down on Colt's shoulder. "You're going to help me with a couple of things before you take off for Mitch's."

Colt grinned. "Only a couple? You usually have a list of things you want me to do that's at least as long as your arm."

She watched as Morgan ushered his brother toward the hall. "Just wait until you drift in home again," he warned with a laugh. "The list will be twice as long." When he reached the door, Morgan turned back to her. "Where do you want us to put the boxes from your car?"

"I'll need to sort through them," she said, trying to remember what they contained. Her and Timmy's clothes had been brought into the house weeks ago, so they wouldn't need to bring the boxes upstairs. "I think most of what's left are kitchen items. Could you put them in the pantry for now?"

Morgan nodded. "Will do."

"Come on, bro," Colt urged. "You can make moon eyes at your wife after I leave."

"You better watch your smart mouth, kid," Morgan said as he followed Colt out into the hall. "I might just have to kick your butt if you don't."

She heard Colt's laughter as the two brothers walked down the hall. "You and whose army?"

As she turned back to empty another dresser drawer, Samantha couldn't help but smile. She enjoyed listening to the good-natured banter between Morgan and his family.

"Samantha?"

At the sound of her name, she looked up to find Colt standing uncertainly at the door. "Where's Morgan? Is something wrong?"

Colt shook his head. "No, everything's fine. Morgan's on his way to the machine shed."

When he continued to stand just inside the room, she asked, "Was there something you needed?"

He shrugged. "I just wanted to thank you."

"For what?" She couldn't imagine why he thought he needed to express his gratitude. To her knowledge, she hadn't done anything that would warrant it.

"Sometimes Brant and I give Morgan a hard time, but he's a good man with a lot of heart. He doesn't think so, but he is." Colt cleared his throat before he continued. "Anyway, I just wanted to thank you for making him happy again."

Before she had a chance to ask what he meant, Colt turned and quickly walked back down the hall, leaving her to stare after him in total bewilderment.

"Is that the last of your clothes?" Morgan asked.

"I think so," Samantha said, looking around the room. She glanced over at the bright red-and-white striped box from the Sleek and Sassy Lady Lingerie Boutique sitting on top of the dresser.

"What's that?"

"Um…it's just…something Annie gave me," she said, her cheeks growing warm. In an effort to change the subject, she pointed to a box of disposable diapers. "Would you mind taking that to your room while I double-check the closet?"

He walked over, took her into his arms and gave her a kiss that left her breathless. "It's *our* room now, sweetheart."

Her stomach fluttered at the look in his startling blue eyes and the suggestive smile curving his firm male lips. "Right. Our room," she said, nodding.

Releasing her, he picked up the carton of diapers. "After I put these with the other baby things, I'll be down in my office for a while. I need to get some paperwork done."

She nodded. "That reminds me. I need to make a list of places to call tomorrow about building estimates and funding for the camp."

"How's it going?"

"Slow." She sighed. "Everyone is either on vacation, or too tied up with other projects to come out to the ranch and give me estimated costs of renovating the house and barn, and building a couple of dormitory cabins."

"It'll all work out, sweetheart," he said, his smile encouraging.

"I hope you're right."

"I am." He started for the door. "After I get a few

things caught up around the ranch, I'll see what I can do to help you.''

Touched by his offer, she smiled. ''Thank you. I'd like that.''

After he left the room, Samantha stared at the empty doorway for several minutes. Morgan Wakefield was indeed a very special man and nothing like her father or Chad. They were selfish, self-centered men, who wouldn't think of offering to help with anything that didn't benefit them in some way.

But Morgan was different. He was kind, thoughtful and went out of his way to do for others—asking nothing for himself in return. He'd offered her his mother's wedding gown when he learned that she really didn't have anything appropriate to wear for the ceremony yesterday. She glanced down at the gold band on her finger. And he'd gone to the trouble and expense of buying wedding rings, so no one would suspect their marriage was anything but the real thing.

Sighing, she sank down on the edge of the bed. She only wished there was something she could do to show him how special she thought he was—something to make him feel as cherished as he'd made her feel in the past few days.

Samantha glanced over at the box Annie had given her the day before. Did she dare try the book and massage oil?

She rose to her feet and walked over to the dresser, lifted the red-and-white striped top and pushed the tissue paper out of the way. Moving the teddy to the side, she dismissed it completely. There wasn't much more to the undergarment than see-through lace and a couple of satin ribbons, and she didn't think she'd ever be able to work up the courage to wear something that provocative.

But Annie had said Brant loved the sensual massage she'd given him on their wedding night. Would Morgan protest his pretend wife giving him one?

Placing the soft, stretchy lace teddy back on top of the book and bottle of oil, Samantha folded the tissue back in place and put the top back on the box. She'd never in a million years have thought of giving a man a sensual massage.

Suppressing a nervous giggle, she shook her head as she tucked the box under her arm and walked from the room. Maybe if she tried really hard, she'd be able to work up the courage to try it sometime. But she wasn't sure she'd ever have the nerve to wear the teddy.

"Samantha?" Morgan tried to open the door to the bathroom adjoining their bedroom. It was locked. "Sweetheart, are you all right?"

He'd held her while she nursed the baby, as he had every night for the past week. But as soon as she'd gotten Timmy to sleep, she'd put him to bed in the cradle over in the corner, disappeared into the bathroom, and Morgan hadn't seen her since. He checked his watch. That had been half an hour ago.

His concern increasing, he pounded on the door.

"Samantha, if you don't answer me, and damned quick, I'm going to break this door down."

"I'm fine, Morgan. I'll be out in a few more minutes," she said, her voice muffled by the thick oak panel separating them. "And keep your voice down. I don't want you waking Timmy."

He frowned as he unbuttoned and removed his shirt, then shucked his jeans and placed them on the chest at the foot of the bed. Walking around to the side, he sat down on the mattress and stared at the bathroom door. What could possibly take a woman that damned long for something as simple as a shower?

As he sat there contemplating the mysterious ways of women, he heard the lock being released. Glancing up, he watched the door open just a crack.

"Morgan?"

He was on his feet and across the room in a flash. "What is it, sweetheart? Are you sure you're all right?"

"Yes, I'm fine. I want you to do something for me," she said, sounding breathless.

"Name it." He tried to push the door open a little wider, but she held it firm.

"I want you to go lay down on the bed."

"You want me to what?" She had him scared about half-spitless and she wanted him to go lay down?

"Dammit, Samantha, what's going on?"

"Just do it, okay?"

"Women," he muttered as he walked back to the bed, shoved the pillows against the headboard, then leaned back against them.

"Are you lying down?"

"Yes," he said, blowing out a frustrated breath. He had no idea what she was up to, but the explanation had better be damned good.

The light in the bathroom went out a split second before the door opened the rest of the way, and Samantha stepped out into the room wearing a shy smile and a scrap of lace that revealed more than it hid.

Morgan sat bolt upright in bed, his eyes wide, his heart thumping his ribs like a bass drum in a high school marching band. "Wh-where..." He had to swallow around the cotton suddenly lining his throat and mouth. "...did you get that?"

"Annie gave it to me on Sunday, just before we got married." An uncertain look replaced her smile. "You don't like it?"

He grinned. "Hell, sweetheart, if I liked it any better, I think I'd probably have a heart attack."

Her easy expression returned as she walked toward him. "I really had no intentions of ever wearing it, but—"

"I'm glad you did, sweetheart," he said, meaning it more than she'd probably ever know.

He started to rise from the bed, but she shook her head and held up her hand. "Would you mind staying there?"

"Why?"

"Because it's taken me almost a week to work up my courage to do this, I'd like to finish," she said, her cheeks turning a pretty shade of rose.

"What do you intend to finish?" he asked, thoroughly intrigued.

He watched her bite her lower lip, then take a deep breath. "I'm going to give you a sensual massage."

Nine

Morgan's heart took off at a gallop and his libido right along with it. ''Sweetheart, are you trying to seduce me?''

Her cheeks colored a very pretty pink. ''Well, no...I mean, I hadn't thought of it that way.''

''It's fine with me if you are. Although, I don't think you can seduce the willing.'' Curious to see what Samantha had in mind, he grinned as he clasped his hands behind his head and leaned back against the pillows. ''But I'm pretty easy to get along with. Go for it.''

Her relieved expression caused his chest to swell with an emotion he forced himself to ignore. He wasn't ready, or willing, to acknowledge anything beyond the fact that his wife was standing before him in nothing more than a wisp of lace and ribbon, and one hell of a sexy smile. And she was looking at him like she fully intended to make him her next meal.

"Keep in mind that I've never done anything like this before, and that I'll have to learn as I go," she said, her throaty admission sending the blood rushing through his veins so fast that it left him light-headed.

"We're breaking new ground here for both of us," he said hoarsely. "You've never given a sensual massage, and I've never gotten one."

She toyed with the tiny satin bow between her breasts. "Do you want me to stop?"

"Hell, no!" He shook his head. "This is just starting to get interesting."

He watched her gaze travel from his face, down his chest to his stomach and beyond. The second she noticed the bulge of his arousal already straining at his briefs, her eyes widened.

"Real interesting," he said, unable to stop grinning. He had no idea what she intended to do next, but he was looking forward to finding out.

When she walked over to the side of the bed, he noticed a bottle in her hand. "What's that?"

"You'll see," she said, her smile sending a curl of heat to the pit of his belly. "But we have to establish a couple of ground rules first."

He made room for her to sit down beside him, then reached for her. "And those would be?"

She drew back. "You can't touch me until I tell you to."

"That's going to be difficult," he said, dropping his arms and feeling as if air was in short supply. "What else?"

"I want you to keep your eyes closed."

This was getting more interesting by the second. "All right. Anything else?"

She gave him a look that sent his blood pressure off the chart. "I want you to concentrate on what I'll be doing to you and tell me how it makes you feel."

He swallowed hard. "You're determined to give me a heart attack, aren't you?"

"No, silly," she said, laughing. "This is supposed to heighten your senses and make you feel wonderful."

"Oh, I'm feeling pretty damned terrific right now as it is," he said, forcing himself to breathe. "And if my senses get any sharper, they could slice granite."

Her smile made the task of lying still all the more difficult. "I hope this makes you feel even better. Now, close your eyes."

When he did as she requested, a pleasant earthy scent drifted around him, followed by something liquid dripping onto his chest. "What is that stuff?"

"Light musk body oil."

"It's…warm." He had to concentrate to keep his eyes shut. "Feels good."

"Mm-hmm. I warmed the bottle in hot water."

She touched him with her soft hands, spreading the

oil over his chest. But when she lightly massaged his pectoral muscles, then circled each one of his flat nipples with the tip of her finger, a shudder ran through him and he sucked in a sharp breath.

"Does that feel good?" she whispered close to his ear.

His muscles flexed and his eyes popped open. "If it felt any better I'd—"

She shook her head. "Close your eyes."

Frowning, he did as she instructed. "Now, I know you're determined to give me a coronary."

He loved the way her hands felt on his body. But he had a feeling before she was finished, he might end up certifiably insane.

As her hands drifted lower over his ribs, to his abdomen and his flanks, she asked, "What are you feeling now?"

Couldn't she tell? Hadn't she noticed how hard his body had become with wanting her?

He had to take a deep breath before he could manage to make his vocal cords work. "I think there's enough electricity running through me right now that I could light up Laramie and probably Cheyenne."

Her throaty laughter only increased the tension building inside of him. "Try to relax."

It was his turn to laugh. "Why don't you ask me to move a couple of mountains while I'm at it?"

"Impossible, huh?"

Shaking his head, he doubled both hands into tight fists to keep from reaching for her. "Never underestimate a man as charged up as I am right now. Just tell me which mountain, when you want it moved and where.''

''I'll give that some thought,'' she said, taking one of her talented little hands away from his lower stomach.

He wondered what she was doing, but the sound of the flip-top cap on the bottle being opened quickly drew his attention. Where was she going to put the oil now?

It didn't take long to find out what she had planned next when he felt the warm liquid dribble over his legs. She placed a hand on each one of his shins, then started spreading the oil upward. His heart stalled. But when she moved her hands over his knees and up his thighs, his pulse took off at breakneck speed and the heat in his lower belly ignited into a flame. If she didn't stop, and damned quick, her hands were going to be dangerously close to—

His eyes snapped open and he swallowed hard. There was no doubt in his mind that she was going to kill him before the night was over. But, he decided as the back of her hand brushed the bulge of his arousal straining against his cotton briefs, he'd leave this world a very happy man.

Unable to lie still a minute longer, Morgan caught her hands in his and drew her up to face him. ''Sweetheart, don't get me wrong. I'm loving the hell out of this seduction business. But I'm about to go into sensory overload.''

Lying across his chest, she smiled down at him. "Don't you want me to finish?"

The air in his lungs came out in one big whoosh and a surge of need arrowed straight to his groin. "If you keep running your hands over me with that warm oil, things will be finished a whole lot sooner than either one of us really wants."

She glanced down his body at the evidence of his overwhelming desire. "Are you trying to tell me that I was successful at giving you a sensual massage?"

If he hadn't been fighting so hard to retain what little control he had left, he might have laughed. "I'd say it was a resounding success, sweetheart." Taking her into his arms, he rolled over to pin her beneath him. "I'll be more than happy to let you do it again any time you want. But would you mind if we put my complete surrender on hold for now and I took it from here?"

"Why?"

"Because I can't take any more of this." He pressed his lower body against her thigh as he lowered his lips to her ear. "I need to be inside of you, bringing you the same pleasure you're giving me."

"I'd like that," she said, shivering against him. Her warm breath teased the side of his neck, sending an answering shudder coursing through him.

The fire in his belly burned brighter, and unable to resist the lure of her soft lips any longer, Morgan traced their fullness with his tongue. When she sighed and wrapped her arms around his shoulders, he deepened the kiss to stroke her inner recesses and coax her into exploring him. Heaven help him, but he was addicted to the sweet taste of her, the way her reserved response quickly turned into passionate need.

Wanting to touch her, to hold her to him and bury himself deep inside of her, he ran his hands the length of her. The scrap of lace she was wearing looked fantastic on her, but he knew beyond a shadow of doubt that he'd like it better off of her. The only problem was, he couldn't figure out how to get her out of it.

He lifted his head to kiss the tip of her nose. "Don't get me wrong. I like whatever this is you're wearing, but how the hell do I get it off of you."

"It's called a teddy." She kissed his chest, sending a shock-wave right through him. "There are two snaps below, at the—"

Before she could finish telling him where they were located, Morgan quickly found and released the tiny fasteners at the apex of her thighs. After he pulled the stretchy lace up and over her head, he removed his briefs and reached for the foil packet he'd tucked beneath his pillow earlier.

"Morgan?" She took the packet from him. "Would you mind if I—"

Blood rushed through his veins when he realized what she was about to ask. "Go right ahead, sweetheart," he said, lying back against the pillows.

He'd never had a woman help arrange their protection before and he found it was more exciting than he could have ever imagined. Her soft touch on his heated body as she rolled the condom into place almost sent him over the edge.

He reached for her once she had the prophylactic taken care of, but Samantha surprised him when she shook her head and moved to straddle his hips. Holding him captive with her smoldering gaze, Morgan thought the top of his head just might come right off his shoulders as her body slowly consumed his.

Closing his eyes, he gritted his teeth and placed his hands on her hips to keep her still. "Don't...move."

Heat and light danced behind his eyelids like some kind of wild laser show as he fought for control. He'd never in his life been this hot, this fast. His body was urging him to allow Samantha to complete the act of loving him, but he ignored it. He wanted this feeling of being one with her to last forever.

The thought might have scared the hell out of him at any other time. But at the moment, Morgan didn't have the strength to fight it. Didn't even want to.

She leaned down to kiss his chest, his shoulder and his chin, then slowly, surely began to rock against him. His senses honed to a razor-sharp edge, he could tell by the tightness of her body and the passionate glow coloring her porcelain cheeks that she was as turned on as he was.

Holding her shapely hips, he helped her set a pace that quickly had them both close to the edge of fulfillment. Only when he felt her inner muscles cling to him, signaling that her release was imminent, did he abandon the last shred of his control and thrust into her a final time. Her moan of pleasure and the rhythmic tremors coursing through her triggered his own climax, and together they hurtled into the realm of complete and utter ecstasy.

The next morning, Morgan shuffled through the stack of files on his desk. When he came across the purchase option he'd had his lawyer draw up for the Shackley ranch, he tossed it aside. He'd have to shred it, along with some other useless papers. But that would have to wait.

He glanced at the calendar. It was time for his annual drive down to the cemetery just outside of Denver to pay his respects to the woman he'd promised to marry.

Every year since Emily's passing, on the day they were to have been married, he'd faithfully placed flowers on her grave and silently begged her forgiveness for his role in her death. But this year would be different. Today, he'd be making the trip to say his final goodbye to her.

He took a deep breath. He'd lain awake most of the night with Samantha nestled in his arms and he'd done a lot of thinking.

Emily was his past and it was time he let her go. She'd been his best friend as well as his lover, and he had no doubt that if they'd married, they would have made it work.

But for the first time in six long years, he felt ready

to move forward and get on with his life. Samantha was his future now. He wanted her with him for the rest of his life, wanted to help her raise Timmy and share her dream of starting a camp for kids of the foster care system.

As he glanced out the window at the distant Shirley Mountains, he sucked in a sharp breath. Good Lord, he'd fallen in love with her.

The thought should have scared the hell out of him. But as the realization settled in, he smiled.

He'd first been drawn to her bravery and pride. She'd faced giving birth to her son in a ramshackle old ranch house with a depth of courage that had astounded him. Then, when she found out that he'd paid the hospital bill, she'd gathered her pride around her like a coat of armor and informed him that she'd cook his meals and clean his house in order to pay him back.

But as he'd gotten to know her better, he'd also learned how kind and caring she was. She was a wonderful mother to Timmy, and even though she had very little herself, she was determined to take her inheritance and turn it into a place where kids could briefly escape their emotional pain.

She'd even allowed him to feel as if he were a member of her little family when she let him hold her while she nursed the baby. And, if she'd let him, he wanted to be a permanent part of it. But he couldn't do that until he made the trip to Denver.

Smiling at the thought of them being a real family,

he slowly rose from his chair and crossed the room. He needed to get on the road. The sooner he bid farewell to his past, the sooner he could get on with his future.

"Samantha?" he called as he walked across the foyer to the great room.

When he found her in the kitchen, he walked up behind her, wrapped his arms around her waist and pulled her back against him. He loved touching her, loved the way she melted against him. Hell, he just plain loved everything about her.

"Sweetheart, I have to go down to Denver today to take care of some unfinished business." He kissed the side of her neck. "Do you need me to pick up anything for you or the baby?"

She turned in his arms to give him a kiss that damned near knocked his size-13 boots right off his feet. "Would you mind picking up a couple of boxes of diapers?"

He shook his head. "Anything else?"

"I can't think of anything." She kissed him again. "How long will you be gone?"

He hated having to leave, when what he really wanted to do was take her upstairs and show her how much she'd come to mean to him, but he needed to say goodbye to an old friend. "I'll be gone most of the day." Giving her a kiss that left them both gasping for breath, he cupped her cheek with his palm. "When I get back, there's something we need to get settled."

She stared at him for several long seconds. "Could I ask what that would be?"

"You'll see." He kissed her again, then set her away from him. If he didn't put some distance between them, he wouldn't even make it as far as the truck, let alone take off for Denver. "I'll call you on my cell phone when I start home."

When he turned to leave, she asked, "Would you mind if I use the computer in your office? It will probably take most of the day, but I'd like to do an Internet search to find contractors for building estimates and possible sources of funding for the camp."

"Sweetheart, the Lonetree is your home now," he said, placing his Resistol on his head as he opened the back door. "You don't have to ask to use my office or anything in it."

Samantha felt warm all over when Morgan winked at her before closing the door behind him. She had no idea what he wanted to talk about, but she had a few things she needed to say to him when he got back.

Her chest tightened and she gave up trying to deny what she knew in her heart to be true. She'd fallen in love with her new husband.

Considering their agreement, it wasn't the smartest thing she'd ever done, but she wasn't sure she'd ever really had a choice in the matter. The question now was could he ever love her in return?

She knew he wanted her. Of that, there was no

doubt. But could Morgan fall in love with her the way a husband loved his wife?

She wasn't sure. But she had every intention of finding out, because there was no way she could remain on the Lonetree Ranch if it turned out that he couldn't.

Strapping Timmy in the baby carrier, Samantha carried him downstairs, along with the folder containing her plans for building the camp. She needed to make some phone calls for estimates on building materials, as well as do an Internet search on Morgan's computer to see what kind of financial aid was available and how to go about obtaining it.

Entering the office, she set the baby carrier on the deacon's bench close to the desk, then settled herself in the big leather desk chair. The first thing she had to do was to start making appointments with an engineer to come out and inspect the existing structures on her grandfather's ranch. If some of them could be renovated, it would cut down on the overall cost of getting the camp up and running.

Glancing over at Timmy, she smiled. "Now, all I have to do is find where Morgan keeps the phone book. Any ideas?"

At the sound of her voice, Timmy waved his little fist in the air and smacked his lips around the pacifier in his mouth.

She laughed. "In other words, you're on your own, Mom."

The pacifier bobbled as if he agreed with her.

"It has to be here somewhere," she said, standing to search the floor-to-ceiling book shelves beside the desk, then the computer center behind it.

Finally spotting the directory under several legal-size files beside the keyboard, she reached to pull the book from beneath the pile. She sighed heavily when the entire stack of folders fell to the floor.

"Morgan will never trust your mommy in his office again," she said to her now sleeping son.

Disgusted with herself for being so careless, she bent to pick up the scattered papers. But her name on one of the documents caught her attention, and straightening, she scanned its contents.

Her heart skipped several beats and a chilling numbness began to fill her soul. Morgan wanted to buy her grandfather's ranch?

Her legs suddenly feeling as if they would no longer support her, she collapsed onto the chair behind the desk. Why would Morgan have a purchase option drawn up? Even before she learned of the new will, and the terms that had to be met to obtain the property, she'd never indicated that she wanted to sell. On the contrary. She'd told Morgan the first day about her plans to turn the ranch into a camp for foster children.

As she thought about the events of the past couple of months, tears filled her eyes, then ran down her cheeks. How could she have been so stupid?

After she'd explained about the camp, Morgan had

avoided her like the plague. He'd left each morning before she got up and hadn't returned until well after she'd gone to bed each night.

But all that changed the day she met with her grandfather's lawyer and he informed her of the new stipulations placed on her inheritance. Once Morgan learned that the land would be turned over to the BLM if she wasn't married, he couldn't get her to the altar fast enough.

Her breath caught on a sob as she glanced down on the gold band circling her finger. What a fool she'd been.

When she questioned him about why he was willing to put his life on hold for the next two years, she'd taken him at his word and foolishly believed that he only wanted to help her hold on to the property. But instead, he'd married her simply because he'd known that once the land was donated to the BLM he'd never get his hands on it.

She scrunched her eyes shut at the emotional pain tightening her chest. Why had she been so quick to believe in Morgan? Hadn't she learned from her father and Chad that men couldn't be counted on for anything but heartache and grief? That they had their own agenda, that didn't include her?

Unable to sit still another minute, she rose to her feet, quickly picked up the remaining files still scattered on the floor and stacked them on the computer center. Turning back to Morgan's desk, she carefully laid the purchase option where he would be sure to see it, then with trembling fingers, removed her wedding band to place it on top of the document.

Tears blurred her vision and her heart felt as if it shattered into a million pieces when she picked up the baby carrier and started out of the office. As she closed the door behind her, the phone started ringing. She ignored it.

She didn't feel like speaking with anyone, nor did she have time. She had to get her suitcases from the store room and start packing to leave.

Morgan let the phone on the other end of the line ring until the answering machine in his office picked up. Frowning, he left another message for Samantha to call him, then depressed the end button. He'd been trying to reach her since leaving the cemetery three hours ago, but she still wasn't answering. Where the hell was she?

She'd told him this morning that she intended to spend the day working on plans for her camp. Fear gripped his belly as he stared out the windshield of his truck at the road ahead. Had something happened to her or the baby?

He pressed down on the accelerator at the same time he pushed the auto-dial on the cell phone. As soon as Annie answered, he asked, "Is Samantha over there at your place?"

"No. I tried calling her a couple of times today, but the answering machine picked up." His sister-in-law sounded alarmed. "Isn't she with you?"

The knot of fear twisting his gut tightened. "No. I've been trying to get hold of her since I left Denver."

"Where are you now? Do you need me to drive over there?"

"I'm only about six miles from home." He turned the truck off the main road and onto Lonetree land. "I'll get there before you could."

"Morgan, if you need us—"

"I'll let you know." As an afterthought he added, "Thanks, Annie."

"When you find out something, let us know if everything is all right." Annie paused. "I…have some bad news, Morgan."

His anxiety increased. "What is it?"

"Colt's friend, Mitch Simpson, was stomped by a bull last night in Houston." He heard Annie take a shaky breath. "He died in surgery a few hours later."

Morgan groaned from the deep sadness filling him. He liked Mitch and his younger sister, Kaylee. Everyone did.

"How's Colt taking it?" he asked, concerned. Colt and Mitch had been best friends since they'd competed against each other at the National High School Rodeo Finals in their junior year. Colt had to be devastated.

"He's taking it pretty hard—" Annie's voice caught. "But he's going to help Kaylee make arrangements for the funeral, then get Mitch's affairs settled before he comes home."

"Was Brant one of the bullfighters?" Morgan asked, knowing that if he was, his brother would blame himself for not taking the hit for Mitch.

"No, he didn't work the event." Annie sighed. "But he's feeling guilty because he wasn't. He said if he'd been there, he might have been able to do something."

It didn't surprise Morgan one bit that Brant regretted not being there. "Are you two driving down to Oklahoma for the funeral?"

"Yes, we'll leave in the morning."

"Take it easy and tell Brant I said to drive safely," Morgan said. "And give my condolences to Kaylee."

"We will. Don't forget to let us know about Samantha," Annie reminded.

"Will do," Morgan said, ending the call.

He tossed the cell phone onto the seat beside him and drove faster. Hearing about Mitch reminded him of how fleeting life was, and if something had happened to Samantha or the baby, he'd never forgive himself for making the trip to Denver, instead of staying home with her.

By the time he skidded to a halt at the side of the ranch house and killed the engine, Morgan already had his shoulder belt unfastened and the driver's door open. Jumping from the truck, he sprinted up the back porch steps, then threw the kitchen door wide. It crashed back against the log wall, splintering wood and shattering the window in the upper part of the door. He couldn't have cared less. All that mattered was finding his wife and son.

"Samantha?" he shouted.

Nothing.

He rushed down the hall, and taking the stairs two at a time, searched every room on the second floor. They were nowhere to be found.

Going back downstairs, he crossed the great room to the foyer. The door to his office was closed. He hoped like hell she'd taken a break from working on the camp plans to nurse the baby and hadn't answered because she didn't want to upset Timmy, or that she'd fallen asleep.

Morgan knew it was unlikely, but at the moment he was ready to grasp any explanation as long as Samantha and the baby were all right.

But when he entered the office, the knot in his gut tightened. Where the hell could she be?

As he started to leave the room, the late afternoon sun streaming through the windows glinted off something on his desk, causing him to turn back. When his gaze zeroed in on the reflective object, the air lodged in his lungs.

Forcing himself to walk over to the desk for a closer inspection, Morgan's heart felt as if it dropped to his boot tops. Samantha's wedding ring sat on top of the purchase option he'd had his lawyer draw up for her grandfather's land.

Ten

As Samantha cradled her crying son to her, she glanced around the living room of her grandfather's run-down ranch house. Tears blurred her vision once again and she tried not to remember the last night they'd spent here—the night Morgan had helped her give birth to the baby.

He'd been her rock—her source of strength and security that night. And she'd foolishly allowed it to continue, until she'd fallen in love with him.

Her breath caught on a sob. She'd been deeply hurt by her father's abandonment and Chad's refusal to have anything to do with Timmy, but both times she'd gotten over it and moved on with her life. But she wasn't sure she'd ever recover from the devastation of Morgan's betrayal.

Why had she convinced herself that he was every-thing he appeared to be? Why had she allowed him to convince her that he truly wanted to help her keep her inheritance? And why had she allowed herself to fall hopelessly in love with him?

"What's wrong with Timmy?"

At the sound of the familiar baritone, Samantha turned to see Morgan standing in the doorway, look-ing much as he had the first time she'd seen him. His wide-brimmed hat pulled low on his forehead, his stance, the rigid set of his jaw, all spoke volumes about his state of mind.

She'd only seen him this way one other time. The night they met. He'd been angry then. He was angry now.

"This is private property," she said, meeting his dark gaze. "You're trespassing."

He shrugged. "So have me arrested."

Shifting the baby from the cradle of her arm to her shoulder, she nodded. "You can bet I will."

"What are you doing here, Samantha?" At the sound of Morgan's voice, Timmy's crying faded to a whimper. "Is the baby all right?"

Samantha detected the concern in Morgan's voice, and no matter how he felt about her, she knew he cared for her son. "He'll be fine. He's fighting sleep."

Morgan walked over to the fireplace to sit down on the raised stone hearth. "When Timmy goes to sleep, we'll talk."

"No, we won't."

"Yes, we will." He sounded just as firm as she had, and from the determination etched on his handsome face, she knew he wasn't going to budge.

Swaying back and forth, she patted Timmy's small back. "There's nothing to say."

"There's plenty to say." Morgan's scowl darkened. "And by damn, Samantha, you're going to hear me out."

Turning to pace the room, she shook her head. "It won't do any good, so you might as well save your breath."

"Look, Samantha, I've had a hell of a day and I don't feel like arguing with you," he said, sounding tired. "Just before I got home and discovered my wife and son had flown the coop, I got word that Colt's best friend, Mitch, died last night after a bull riding accident."

"Oh, I'm so sorry for Colt's loss," she said, her heart going out to her youngest brother-in-law. "Is Colt all right?"

Morgan shook his head. "Annie said he's taking it pretty hard." Rising to his feet, he looked around. "Where's the baby carrier? Timmy's asleep."

"Over by the couch." She kept her voice low, in order not to disturb her son.

Morgan walked over to take the baby from her, then went back to the couch to gently place her sleeping son in the baby seat. When he straightened to his full height, he turned toward her. "Why don't we go back to the Lonetree to talk this out?"

She shook her head. "I'd rather not."

"Why?"

"I don't belong there," she said, her heart breaking. She'd come to love the Lonetree Ranch, almost as much as she loved its owner, and it broke her heart to think she'd never be going back.

Closing the distance between them, he towered over her. "That's bull and you know it. The Lonetree is your home."

"No, Morgan," she said quietly. "It never was."

"How can you say that, Samantha? You're my wife."

He reached for her, but she stepped back. She couldn't let him touch her. If she did, she wasn't sure she'd have the strength to resist him.

"Let's talk about that, Morgan." She folded her arms beneath her breasts. "Let's discuss the reasons behind your willingness to marry me."

His piercing blue gaze met hers head-on. "You were going to lose your inheritance and—"

"And what?" she interrupted, ignoring the pain caused by his duplicity and letting her anger take control. "You were going to lose any chance of getting your hands on the property?"

He shook his head. "No. *You* were going to lose what was rightfully yours and your dream of opening the camp."

Taking a deep shuddering breath, she met his dark

gaze head-on. "Did you, or did you not, want to buy my grandfather's ranch?"

"I did." He had the audacity to smile. "But I don't anymore."

Her anger increased. "How silly of me to forget such an important detail. There's no longer a need to purchase the land, is there? It came as part of the package when you married me."

"Nope. This is your place." He took a step toward her, but she forced herself to stand her ground.

"Not for much longer." Tears filled her eyes again, but she blinked them away. "Once our divorce is final, it will belong to the BLM."

She watched his smile fade and a muscle begin to twitch along his firm jaw. "We're not getting a divorce," he said firmly.

"Yes, we are," she insisted.

"*No,* we're not." Morgan took a step forward. "We're going to stay married, in two years you're going to get the title to your land and start your camp for foster kids."

"I can't do that."

"Why not?"

"Because we aren't going to stay married long enough for me to get the land," she repeated.

He sighed heavily. "This is getting us absolutely nowhere. What do you say we start over?"

Her stubborn little chin came up defiantly. "What's the point?"

As she stared at him, he could see myriad emotions

in the depths of her whiskey-colored eyes. He hated that his carelessness had hurt her and caused her distress, but he had to explain. Their future together depended on it.

Reaching out, he touched her cheek with his index finger. "Just hear me out, Samantha. Please."

"At this point, I doubt there will be anything you could say that will change things," she said, suddenly sounding tired. "But if it will get you to leave, then fine. I'll listen."

"Fair enough." He gave her what he hoped was an encouraging smile. "Do you remember the day you and Timmy came home from the hospital and I suggested that you sell this place?"

"Yes, but I thought you were talking about listing it with a Realtor." She walked over to the hearth to sit down. "You didn't tell me you were the one interested in buying the property."

"No, I didn't." Morgan paused. He needed to choose his words carefully. This was too important to have any more misunderstandings between them. "I had called my attorney to draw up the purchase option before I talked to you about selling it. But once I learned of your plans, I didn't see any reason to mention it. Starting a camp for kids is a much better use for the land than my just wanting to make the Lonetree bigger."

"Then why didn't you destroy the document if you didn't think at some later date you could convince me to sell?" she asked, looking doubtful.

"Because I'm a fool," he said, shaking his head at his own carelessness. "I had the attorney mail it to me so I didn't get it until a week or two after we'd talked. By that time, I was busy working from daylight until well after dark. I was so tired when it arrived, I opened the envelope, saw what it was, then tossed it on a stack of files and forgot about it. Then, when I ran across it this morning, I put it on a stack of papers I need to destroy."

"Okay, I'll accept that. But once you found out about my plans for the camp, you avoided me like the plague," she said, clearly unconvinced. "Then, when you learned that I was about to lose my ranch to the BLM because I wasn't married, you couldn't get me to the altar fast enough. Why?"

Her chin rose another notch and he couldn't help but smile. She was cute as hell when she was angry.

"You don't have a clue about the relationship between ranchers and the BLM, do you, sweetheart?"

"No, I...what does that have to do with anything?" She didn't look quite as certain as she had only moments ago.

"I could have had the land by the first of next year, if I hadn't married you."

"Oh, really?" She didn't look like she believed him. "And how would you have managed that?"

"All I would have had to do was contact the office in Casper and arrange for a long-term lease." He shrugged. "The land would have been mine for as long as I cared to pay for its use."

He could tell she was considering his explanation. ''Then you really did marry me to help me keep my land?'' she asked, her voice little more than a whisper.

Morgan nodded. ''Among other reasons.''

He watched the anger and hurt in her pretty amber eyes turn to bewilderment. ''What other reasons?''

Taking a deep breath, Morgan knew the time had come to lay it all on the line. ''I tried to stay away from you as much as possible because I couldn't keep my hands off of you,'' he said, hoping she'd understand. ''You were everything I wanted, but couldn't have.''

''What do you mean I was everything you couldn't have?'' she asked, looking more confused than ever.

As he tried to find the words to tell her why he felt the way he had, he rubbed the back of his neck in an effort to relieve some of his tension. This was possibly the most important discussion he'd ever have in his entire life and he hoped like hell that he didn't blow it.

Deciding there was no better way to tell her about his past than straight out, he walked over to sit down beside her on the hearth. ''Six years ago, I was engaged to be married. But a week before the wedding, I talked my fiancée into visiting her sister down in Denver while I caught up on chores around the ranch. She didn't want to go, but I insisted.'' He loosely clasped his hands between his knees and stared down at them. ''While they were out shopping, she and her sister were caught in the cross fire between the police and a couple of thugs trying to rob a jewelry store. She...died instantly.''

''Oh, Morgan, I'm so sorry,'' she said, placing her hand on his arm. ''That must have been awful for you.''

He nodded, but remained silent for several moments, drawing comfort from Samantha's warm touch. Covering her hand with his, he finished, ''After that, I vowed that I would never make decisions for another person I cared about. No matter what the circumstances.''

''It wasn't your fault, Morgan,'' she said, her voice filled with compassion.

''Whether it was, or not, I still felt responsible.''

Samantha watched Morgan closely. She could tell that he'd been deeply affected by the loss of his fiancée. ''Do you still feel that way?'' she asked, quietly.

Turning to face her, he shrugged one shoulder. ''I guess I'll always blame myself to a certain extent. But I finally feel ready to move on. It's the reason I made the trip to Denver today. I had to put flowers on her grave and say goodbye.'' He stopped to clear his throat. ''I want us to stay together, Samantha.''

Her breath caught, and for the first time since he walked in the door, hope began to blossom within her. ''Why, Morgan? Is it just because you want to help me get my land?''

''No.'' She watched him glance down at his hands,

then take a deep breath before he raised his head to look at her. "I want to hold you every night and wake up with you in my arms each morning for the rest of my life, Samantha. I already think of Timmy as my own son. I want to adopt him and help you raise him."

Tears filled her eyes and her heart skipped several beats. "Really?"

He nodded. "I also want to help you start your camp."

After all of the things he said he wanted for their life together, she was sure Morgan loved her. But she needed to hear the words. "Why?"

"Because I...love you," he said, his voice rough with emotion. He reached into his shirt pocket to remove something, then taking her left hand in his, he slipped her wedding band back onto her finger.

When he wrapped his strong arms around her and buried his face in her hair, she felt as if her heart would burst with happiness. "Oh, Morgan, I love you, too."

He held her for several minutes before he spoke again. "I can't live without you, sweetheart. Please don't ever leave me again."

She shook her head. "Never."

Releasing her, he cupped her face with his large hands. "I want you to understand that even though we'll be a family, and equal partners in our marriage, I won't make any decisions, or try to persuade you to do anything you don't want to do."

Her chest tightened with emotion at the sincerity she saw in his brilliant blue eyes. He was such a good man, and one that she knew would never do anything to intentionally hurt or disappoint her, or Timmy, if it was within his power to prevent it.

"Morgan, darling, I hate to be the one to break this to you," she said, touching his jaw with her fingertips. "But you've been making decisions for me since the moment we met."

Frowning, he shook his head. "No, I haven't."

"Yes, you have." She couldn't keep from smiling. "You took charge as soon as you found out I was in labor and told me that I couldn't take myself to the hospital."

"That was different."

"How?"

"You were in no shape to drive."

"That's right. But you didn't give me a choice, did you?" When he slowly shook his head, she continued, "And what about your insistence that Timmy and I stay at the Lonetree with you, instead of coming back here?"

She could tell he considered her words before he finally spoke. "This place doesn't have heat, water or electricity. It wouldn't have been good for you or the baby."

"Once again, you were looking out for our welfare," she said, nodding. "You assessed the situation and *decided* it wasn't a good environment for us. You took care of us, Morgan."

He seemed to mull that over for a moment before he grinned sheepishly. "I guess I did, didn't I?"

She nodded. "Morgan?"

"What, sweetheart?"

"There's a few things that I want from our marriage, too," she said.

Giving her a quick kiss, he smiled. "Name it, sweetheart."

"Promise me that you'll continue to watch out for me and Timmy," she said smiling.

Nodding, he ran his thumb over the gold band around her finger as his brilliant blue gaze met hers. "I'll protect you both with my life. Anything else?"

"How do you feel about having more children?" she asked. "I'd like for Timmy to have a couple of brothers and sisters."

His serious expression easing, he laughed. "Sweetheart, I'll be more than happy to give you all the babies you want. Is that all?"

She nodded, the love she felt for him blossoming inside of her with each passing second. "Take us home, Morgan."

He stared at her for endless seconds. "I love you, Samantha. Once I take you back to the Lonetree, I don't ever intend to let you go. This marriage will be forever."

"I love you with all my heart and soul, Morgan," she said, tears filling her eyes. "That's what I want, too."

Giving her a kiss that sent her heart soaring, he

stood up. Then smiling, took her hand in his and pulled her up to stand beside him. "Forever, sweetheart."

She nodded as she smiled back at him. "Forever."

Epilogue

Two years later

"**O**ut, Daddy! Out!"

Morgan smiled as he unfastened the safety straps on Timmy's car seat and lifted him out of the truck cab. "Let's go see what Mommy's doing," he said, setting his son on his feet.

"Mommy! We here," Timmy yelled, racing toward the ranch house they'd turned into an office for Camp Safe Haven as fast as his short little legs would allow.

When he reached the steps, Morgan reminded, "Be careful and hold on to the rail."

Stepping out onto the porch, Samantha laughed

when Timmy knocked his black cowboy hat off when he raised his arm to take hold of the wooden banister. "How are my two favorite Wakefield men?"

"We here," Timmy said proudly.

Morgan grinned as he helped Timmy put his hat back on, then helped him up the steps. "We're doing pretty good. After Timmy coerced Uncle Colt into taking him for a horseback ride, he helped me feed Stormy Gal's new colt, then we went over to visit Uncle Brant, Aunt Annie and little Zach."

"It sounds like you've had a full morning," she said as she lowered herself into one of the rocking chairs by the door, then lifted Timmy onto her lap.

"You feeling all right?" Morgan asked, sitting in the chair beside her.

Nodding, she started rocking Timmy who looked as if he might fall asleep at any moment. "I'm fine." She grinned. "No backaches, no contractions, nothing."

When Morgan placed his hand on her rounded stomach, the baby inside kicked as if telling his father "hello." He laughed. "I see our little football player is still practicing his punting skills."

"He's definitely been active today," she agreed, rubbing the spot where the baby had poked her. "By the way, did you call to see if Kaylee Simpson would be interested in being the riding instructor when camp opens next week?"

"I e-mailed her, but she's not interested." He shook his head. "She said that she hasn't ridden in some time and doesn't intend to. She's out of school now and working as a physical trainer.'' He frowned. ''I got the feeling she doesn't want to have anything to do with any of us.''

''Do you think Brant would be interested in the job?''

Grinning, he nodded. ''Since Annie is going to be the activity director, and here everyday, I'm betting he'll be here anyway.''

''Go-o-o-d,'' she said, drawing out the word in a way that caused his heart to stall.

''Samantha?''

''What time is it?''

''Was that—''

He watched her focus her gaze on his truck for several long seconds. The hair on the back of his neck stood straight up. Unless he missed his guess, he was going to be a daddy again soon. Real soon.

When she blew out a deep breath, then turned to smile at him, he knew he'd never in his life forget how beautiful she was at that very moment, or how very much he loved her. ''Morgan, I think we'd better take Timmy over to spend the night with Brant and Annie.''

Rising to his feet, Morgan took their sleeping son in his arms and helped the woman he loved more than life itself to her feet. ''Let's get going.''

She looked absolutely radiant and he was once again struck by her calm, and the depth of her courage. "What's the matter, darling? Don't you want to deliver this baby like you did Timmy?"

"Sweetheart, that was a one time shot," he said, locking the office door and helping her down the steps. "I'm more than happy to be your birthing coach, but that's as far as it goes. This time, you're going to be in the hospital with doctors who know what the hell they're doing."

"I love you, Morgan Wakefield," she said, placing her soft hand along his jaw.

He gazed at the woman who had given him everything he'd ever wanted in life—a family and a home filled with love and laughter. "And I love you, sweetheart," he said, turning his head to kiss her palm. "More than you'll ever know."

*   *   *   *   *

Don't miss Kathie DeNosky's
next Silhouette Desire,
LONETREE RANCHERS: COLT,
available December 2003.

Silhouette Desire

is proud to present
an exciting new miniseries from

KATHIE DeNOSKY

Lonetree Ranchers

On the Lonetree Ranch, passions explode
under Western skies for these
handsome-but-hard-to-tame bachelors.

In August 2003—
LONETREE RANCHERS: BRANT

In October 2003—
LONETREE RANCHERS: MORGAN

In December 2003—
LONETREE RANCHERS: COLT

Available at your favorite retail outlet.

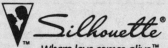

Silhouette

Where love comes alive™

✂

Your opinion is important to us! Please take a few moments to share your thoughts with us about your experiences with Harlequin and Silhouette books. Your comments will be very useful in ensuring that we deliver books you love to read.
***Please take a few minutes to complete the questionnaire,
then send it to us at the address below.***

Send your completed questionnaires to:
Harlequin/Silhouette Reader Survey, P.O. Box 9046, Buffalo, NY 14269-9046

1. As you may know, there are many different lines under the Harlequin and Silhouette brands. Each of the lines is listed below. Please check the box that most represents your reading habit for each line.

Line	Currently read this line	Do not read this line	Not sure if I read this line
Harlequin American Romance	❑	❑	❑
Harlequin Duets	❑	❑	❑
Harlequin Romance	❑	❑	❑
Harlequin Historicals	❑	❑	❑
Harlequin Superromance	❑	❑	❑
Harlequin Intrigue	❑	❑	❑
Harlequin Presents	❑	❑	❑
Harlequin Temptation	❑	❑	❑
Harlequin Blaze	❑	❑	❑
Silhouette Special Edition	❑	❑	❑
Silhouette Romance	❑	❑	❑
Silhouette Intimate Moments	❑	❑	❑
Silhouette Desire	❑	❑	❑

2. Which of the following best describes why you bought *this book?* One answer only, please.

the picture on the cover	❑	the title	❑
the author	❑	the line is one I read often	❑
part of a miniseries	❑	saw an ad in another book	❑
saw an ad in a magazine/newsletter	❑	a friend told me about it	❑
I borrowed/was given this book	❑	other: _____	❑

3. Where did you buy *this book?* One answer only, please.

at Barnes & Noble	❑	at a grocery store	❑
at Waldenbooks	❑	at a drugstore	❑
at Borders	❑	on eHarlequin.com Web site	❑
at another bookstore	❑	from another Web site	❑
at Wal-Mart	❑	Harlequin/Silhouette Reader	❑
at Target	❑	Service/through the mail	
at Kmart	❑	used books from anywhere	❑
at another department store or mass merchandiser	❑	I borrowed/was given this book	❑

4. On average, how many Harlequin and Silhouette books do you buy at one time?

I buy _____ books at one time	❑
I rarely buy a book	❑

MRQ403SD-1A

5. How many times per month do you shop for any *Harlequin and/or Silhouette* books?
   One answer only, please.

1 or more times a week	❏	a few times per year	❏
1 to 3 times per month	❏	less often than once a year	❏
1 to 2 times every 3 months	❏	never	❏

6. When you think of your ideal heroine, which *one* statement describes her the best?
   One answer only, please.

She's a woman who is strong-willed	❏	She's a desirable woman	❏
She's a woman who is needed by others	❏	She's a powerful woman	❏
She's a woman who is taken care of	❏	She's a passionate woman	❏
She's an adventurous woman		She's a sensitive woman	❏

7. The following statements describe types or genres of books that you may be
   interested in reading. Pick *up to 2 types* of books that you are most interested in.

I like to read about truly romantic relationships	❏
I like to read stories that are sexy romances	❏
I like to read romantic comedies	❏
I like to read a romantic mystery/suspense	❏
I like to read about romantic adventures	❏
I like to read romance stories that involve family	❏
I like to read about a romance in times or places that I have never seen	❏
Other: _____	❏

*The following questions help us to group your answers with those readers who are
similar to you. Your answers will remain confidential.*

8. Please record your year of birth below.
   19 _____

9. What is your marital status?
   single ❏   married ❏   common-law ❏   widowed ❏
   divorced/separated ❏

10. Do you have children 18 years of age or younger currently living at home?
    yes ❏   no ❏

11. Which of the following best describes your employment status?
    employed full-time or part-time ❏   homemaker ❏   student ❏
    retired ❏   unemployed ❏

12. Do you have access to the Internet from either home or work?
    yes ❏   no ❏

13. Have you ever visited eHarlequin.com?
    yes ❏   no ❏

14. What state do you live in?
    _____

15. Are you a member of Harlequin/Silhouette Reader Service?
    yes ❏   Account # _____   no ❏   MRQ403SD-1B

From
Katherine Garbera

CINDERELLA'S CHRISTMAS AFFAIR

Silhouette Desire #1546

With the help of a matchmaking
angel in training, two ugly-ducklings-
turned-swans experience passion and
love…and a little holiday magic.

You're on his hit list.

*Available November 2003
at your favorite retail outlet.*

COMING NEXT MONTH

#1543 WITH PRIVATE EYES—Eileen Wilks
Dynasties: The Barones

Socialite Claudia Barone *insisted* on helping investigate the attempted sabotage of her family's business. But detective Ethan Mallory had a hard head to match his hard body. He always worked on his own....he didn't need the sexy sophisticate on the case. What he *wanted*...well, that was another matter!

#1544 BABY, YOU'RE MINE—Peggy Moreland
The Tanners of Texas

In one moment, Woodrow Tanner changed Dr. Elizabeth Montgomery's life. The gruff-yet-sexy rancher had come bearing news of her estranged sister's death—and the existence of Elizabeth's baby niece. Even as Elizabeth tried to accept this startling news, she couldn't help but crave Woodrow's consoling embrace....

#1545 WILD IN THE FIELD—Jennifer Greene
The Lavender Trilogy

Like the fields of lavender growing outside her window, Camille Campbell looked sweet and delicate, but could thrive even in the harshest conditions. Divorced dad and love-wary neighbor Pete MacDougal found in Camille a kindred soul...whose body could elicit in him the most amazing feelings....

#1546 CINDERELLA'S CHRISTMAS AFFAIR—Katherine Garbera
King of Hearts

Brawny businessman Tad Randolph promised his parents he'd be married with children before Christmas—and cool-as-ice executive CJ Terrance was the perfect partner for his pretend wedding and baby-making scheme. But soon Tad realized she was more fire than ice...and found himself wishing CJ shared more than just his bed!

#1547 ENTANGLED WITH A TEXAN—Sara Orwig
Texas Cattleman's Club: The Stolen Baby

A certain sexy rancher was the stuff of fantasies for baby store clerk Marissa Wilder. So when David Sorrenson showed up needing Marissa's help, she quickly agreed to be a temporary live-in nanny for the mystery baby David was caring for. But could she convince her fantasy man to care for *her*, as well?

#1548 AWAKENING BEAUTY—Amy J. Fetzer

There was more to dowdy bookseller Lane Douglas than met the eye...and Tyler McKay was determined to find out her secrets. Resisting the magnetic millionaire was difficult for Lane, but she vowed to keep her identity under wraps...even as her heart and body threatened to betray her.

SDCNM1003